"ARE YOU IN LOVE WITH THAT HARPER FELlow you're seeing?" Kane demanded, closing one hand around her wrist.

"What business is that of yours?" Mel asked.

"I'm making it my business."

She tried to pull free but couldn't. "He's a good man, and we have similar interests."

Kane pulled her closer. "Does he make your toes curl when he makes love to you?"

Her first instinct was to slap him. Mel raised her hand to do just that, but he caught it. "You are clearly out of line," she said fiercely.

"You saved me," he said. "I feel it's my duty to return the favor." Still holding both her hands, he pulled her against him. Her mouth flew open in protest, and he used it to his advantage, capturing her lips and kissing her hungrily, greedily, leaving no doubt as to how much he wanted her.

When he finally released her, Mel stared at him. She had never, ever been kissed like that before. "Who do you think you are?" she demanded, trembling from head to toe. "What gives you the right?"

He offered her a cocky smile, but his insides were shaking from needing her so much. "Nobody gave me the right to kiss you. I took it 'cause I figured you needed kissing." He paused and fixed her with a lethal smile. "And if you don't leave right now, I'm going to kiss you again. . . ."

WHAT ARE *LOVESWEPT* ROMANCES?

They are stories of true romance and touching emotion. We believe those two very important ingredients are constants in our highly sensual and very believable stories in the LOVESWEPT line. Our goal is to give you, the reader, stories of consistently high quality that may sometimes make you laugh, sometimes make you cry, but are always fresh and creative and contain many delightful surprises within their pages.

Most romance fans read an enormous number of books. Those they truly love, they keep. Others may be traded with friends and soon forgotten. We hope that each LOVESWEPT romance will be a treasure—a "keeper." We will always try to publish

LOVE STORIES YOU'LL NEVER FORGET
BY AUTHORS YOU'LL ALWAYS REMEMBER

The Editors

Loveswept ® 684

THE DEVIL AND MISS GOODY TWO-SHOES

CHARLOTTE HUGHES

BANTAM BOOKS
NEW YORK · TORONTO · LONDON · SYDNEY · AUCKLAND

THE DEVIL AND MISS GOODY TWO-SHOES
A Bantam Book / May 1994

*If you would be interested in receiving protective vinyl covers for your
Loveswept books, please write to this address for information:*

> Loveswept
> Bantam Books
> P.O. Box 985
> Hicksville, NY 11802

ISBN 0-553-44391-7

Published simultaneously in the United States and Canada

PRINTED IN THE UNITED STATES OF AMERICA

OPM   0 9 8 7 6 5 4 3 2 1

To Susann Brailey
for all your help

ONE

Kane Stoddard cut the engine on his battered Harley, shoved the kickstand in place with the heel of his boot, and read the address on the rustic frame building once more. As he climbed off his bike, he could still feel the vibrations from the powerful engine rumbling through his body. His right hand ached from having gripped the throttle for so many hours. His shoulder muscles were sore. He didn't care. It felt good to use all the parts of his body.

Prison had taught him to appreciate the simple things.

He sucked his breath in deeply and tasted the crisp Mississippi air. It was fresh and clean with no lingering scents of urine and disinfectant. Spring. How fitting to be given a new start in life when everything around him was coming alive as well.

He smiled, then realized it was the first time

he'd smiled in months. Not that he'd had a whole lot to smile about these past three years. But, out of the blue, everything had changed. The warden had called him into his office to apologize for the terrible mistake they'd made, *they* being the judicial system that Kane had long ago lost respect for—the *same* system that put bank robbers behind bars for forty-five years and gave child molesters ten.

"I've wonderful news for you, Mr. Stoddard," the warden had said, as if addressing inmates respectfully took the sting out of all the other humiliations they were forced to endure. "A man fitting your description robbed a Memphis convenience store a couple of weeks ago. The clerk shot him in the chest. As the man lay dying, he confessed to several crimes, including the one for which you were convicted." The warden paused. "His story checked out. He knew details about the crime that only the police knew."

Now, three days after his release, as Kane stood before Abercrombie Grocery, he thought of the bundle of letters in his duffel bag that had led him to Hardeeville, Mississippi.

Melanie Abercrombie had begun writing to him a year earlier when she'd received his name from her pastor. Kane suspected the preacher hoped his congregation would bring a few criminals to salvation. Well, Miss Abercrombie hadn't saved his soul, but she'd certainly made the small Mississippi town and its occupants sound interesting. Through her letters,

Kane knew the good Reverend Potts had a weakness for rhubarb pie, his wife a fondness for gossip. He'd also read about the Babcocks, who owned the local bakery and often left their loaf bread and rolls on the shelves too long instead of moving them to the"thrift" section and marking them half-price. *This*, Miss Abercrombie declared, was probably due to the fact that their teenage daughter, Desiree, refused to buy her clothes at the moderately priced Aaronson's Department Store like everyone else, preferring the new mall in the next town instead. It was no wonder folks in Hardeeville were being forced to pay top dollar for stale bread.

Kane had read each and every letter, sometimes three or four times before tucking them into the shoe box beneath his cot. He'd never answered them, of course, not only because he couldn't think of a damn thing to say to the woman but because he didn't want anyone to think the letters were important. The minute someone found out something mattered, they took it away.

Nevertheless, he had found himself wondering about Melanie Abercrombie: what she looked like, the sound of her voice. She had to have a pretty voice, because she'd mentioned singing in the church choir. As for looks, she was probably as plain as a dust mop, he'd convinced himself. Otherwise, she wouldn't spend all her free time writing to him.

Kane pulled his duffel bag from the bike and

approached the store, trying to decide if it looked as Melanie Abercrombie had described it. The building had to be at least a hundred years old, the wood faded and warped in places from the weather. A vintage soda-pop machine shared space with two long benches on the front porch, where a faded green awning offered relief from the elements. Double screen doors marked the entrance, both of which sagged and looked as though they'd come completely unhinged in the next strong wind. Beside one door a small sign listed the hours of operation. A sign on the other side of the doors listed the rules. *No loitering, profanity, or alcoholic beverages allowed.* Kane didn't have to be psychic to know who'd put up the sign. Even in her letters, Miss Melanie Abercrombie had come across as a real lady.

He paused before the door, suddenly nervous at the thought of meeting the woman who'd written to him faithfully the past year. How would she react when she saw him for the first time? His release had come about so quickly, he hadn't had a chance to notify her.

Melanie Abercrombie was in a sour mood, brought on by hunger pangs, her younger sister's desperate, incessant phone calls, and a feeling of being overwhelmed. She peered through clunky square-framed glass at the mess before her.

Abercrombie Grocery was as disorganized and cluttered as a child's playroom, proof that her father preferred visiting with his customers and listening to gospel music to sweeping and restocking shelves. Mel ran a finger across the lid of a jar of pickled beets where a layer of dust and grime had long since settled and made it impossible to read the price.

She knew she was partially responsible for the mess. Her flower shop had been in an uproar for a solid month, what with Easter, Secretaries' Day, and proms following one right after the other. It was so bad her assistant, Eunice Jenkins, claimed she was getting varicose veins from standing on her feet so long and prickly heat from handling pom-poms. Mel simply hadn't had time to come by her father's store and clean the way she usually did. It was no wonder folks were driving into town to shop at the new Thrifty Sak.

Nevertheless, Mel had had no idea how bad business had been until she looked through her father's financial records. Only then did she realize they would have to take desperate measures. The store *must* be cleaned up once and for all. They'd have to pull up all that scarred linoleum and tear down the warped shelves. They'd have to patch the roof over the meat cooler and repair the faucet on the bathroom sink and have someone look at the old oil heater at the back that never quite kept the place warm enough in winter.

Mel sighed heavily. It was going to take so much

time and money, neither of which she had very much of these days.

That brought her to the next problem: Where the heck was the carpenter she'd hired to *do* the work? She groaned inwardly as she wondered about him. She'd hired the man sight unseen from a classified in the newspaper stating he was unemployed and would work cheap. She'd later learned, through the grapevine at church, that the fellow was unemployed due to a tendency to drink and forget about work altogether.

Mel was interrupted from her thoughts when one of the screen doors was thrown open and a man stepped through.

"Melanie Abercrombie?" he asked, trying to make himself heard above a modern rendition of "Jesus Loves Me" coming from a radio at the back of the store.

At first all Mel could do was stare at him.

She felt her jaw drop clear to her collar as she regarded the man before her. His head and face were covered with snarled blue-black hair. His eyes were just as black; his look hard, flat, and emotionless. It was the sort of face one expected to find on Wanted posters, the sort of face that prompted decent folks to lock their doors at night before they went to bed.

So *this* was her carpenter. No wonder he couldn't keep a job.

"Well, it's about time you got here," she said, her

voice as crisp as fried salt pork. She wasn't going to allow herself to be put off by that beard. She took in his clothes, the blue sweat-stained work shirt, and shamefully tight jeans. He looked tough, lean, and sinewy. "I've been waiting for you all day."

"You have?" Kane was clearly surprised. He couldn't imagine how she'd learned he was getting out.

"Yes," she replied, noting he didn't look the least bit remorseful for being so late. Didn't he *want* the job, for heaven's sake? "I suppose an apology is out of the question," she said.

He went blank. "You can apologize if you want, but I certainly don't expect it."

Her irritation flared. "I wasn't talking about *me* apologizing to *you*," she said tightly.

His bafflement quickly turned to annoyance. She had obviously called the prison, although he couldn't imagine why. She had never once tried to contact him by phone. "Why should *I* apologize?" he asked. "I came as quickly as I could. Hell, I don't even have to be here."

"Oh, is that right?" she quipped, staring straight into his lethal black eyes. She paused. "You think I'm desperate, don't you?"

He was growing more confused. "Come again?"

"That's it, isn't it?" She fidgeted with the buttons on her blouse. "You think I need you so badly that I'll put up with this sort of behavior."

Kane was truly at a loss as he studied the woman before him and wondered where in the hell the conversation was going. "I don't think you're desperate," he said, at the same time wondering if she expected him to court her in return for all those letters. She was clearly not his type. Her skirt and blouse were too prim and proper; her hairstyle—slicked back into a bun—too severe. Her glasses were downright ugly and made her face appear misshapen. "I don't want to a appear rude, Miss Abercrombie, but I'm not looking to get romantically involved with *anyone* right now. I'm just looking to make a fresh start."

"What?" Mel's head spun. What in blazes was he talking about? Did he think she was making a pass at him? Was he insane? She opened her mouth to speak, but he cut her off.

"Look, I don't want us to get off to a bad beginning. I'm not sure I would have made it this past year without your letters." It wasn't easy for him to be so honest, but she had done much for his morale these twelve months; he owed her.

Mel was at a loss. He wasn't making sense. "Letters? What letters? Who *are* you?"

"Kane Stoddard."

She froze as realization swept through her with the force of a tidal wave. "Kane Stoddard? From Leavenworth?" He nodded, and she thought she detected a small smile, but it was hard to tell with the beard.

"But how can that be?" she asked herself out loud. The Kane Stoddard she knew was a convicted killer, serving life without parole. How had he gotten out? The answer came to her with lightning-quick clarity. She knew of only one way a prisoner could get out that fast.

Kane watched the color drain from her face. He had expected her to be surprised, but she looked as if she'd just received the scare of her life. "Are you okay?" he asked.

She knew she ought to do something, but what? Dial 911? Race outside and flag down the first motorist who came along? She tried to move, but her feet felt as though they'd been set in cement.

An escaped convict in Hardeeville? Was it possible?

Kane watched, transfixed, as Melanie Abercrombie's eyes glazed over, then rolled back in her head like dice in a card game. She swayed, and he reached for her. He wasn't fast enough. She collapsed and fell against a box of drain cleaner with the grace and finesse of a hundred-pound gunny sack of Vidalia onions.

TWO

It was all Kane could do to keep her from injuring herself in the fall. Her head barely missed the sharp-edged counter, and he caught her a split second before she hit the floor. He couldn't save the glasses. They landed hard, shattering both lenses. He figured it was to her advantage.

"Somebody help me," Kane called out, not knowing what to do with the dead weight in his arms. Suddenly, the music at the other end of the store died. A stocky, square-faced man with gray hair stepped out from behind the meat case, took one look at the situation, and raced forward.

"What happened to my daughter?" he demanded in a voice that told Kane he'd better not be responsible.

Still clutching an unconscious Melanie Abercrombie against him, Kane lowered her gently to the floor while cradling her head with one arm. "I don't know. One minute she seemed fine, the next thing I know she's out cold. Help me find something to put under her head."

Wilton Abercrombie stripped off his apron, wadded it into a ball, and tucked it beneath his daughter's head. He patted her face gently with meaty hands. "Wake up, Mel, honey," he said. "Open your eyes."

The woman on the floor stirred.

"I think she's coming around," Kane said. "Miss Abercrombie?" Her eyelids fluttered open, and Kane noticed for the first time how green her eyes were.

Mel blinked at the dark-haired man several times. "What happened?"

"You fainted."

She touched her temples. "And my glasses?"

Kane reached for them. "They didn't survive the fall." He noted the perfect oval face, the clear green eyes. "You ask me, I think it's a blessing." He paused. "Why'd you faint? Are you sick?"

Mel pushed herself up into a sitting position, brushing her skirt into place and praying the man had not caught a glimpse of her unmentionables. She wondered how she was going to come up with the money for new glasses but was more concerned at the moment with the possibility of having an escaped convict on her hands. "I never get sick," she replied, as if falling prey to an ailment were a sign of weak character. She would not let him see that she was frightened. "I was just surprised to see you, Mr. Stoddard," she managed. "I had no idea you were—" She paused. "That you had left your *other* place."

Kane caught on quickly. She obviously didn't want her father to know he was an ex-con. "Neither did I. It sort of happened at the *last minute*," he said, emphasizing the words so maybe she'd understand why he hadn't notified her. He saw the funny look she gave him and wondered at it.

"Do you two know each other?" Wilton Abercrombie asked.

"This is Kane Stoddard, Daddy. From Kansas," Mel added. "We've been writing to each other for about a year."

Wilton took the younger man's hand and pumped it enthusiastically, as though he didn't find it at all strange that his daughter had been corresponding with a man who looked like a refugee from a soup kitchen. "What part of Kansas?" he asked.

Kane was the first to pull his hand away. Prison had taught him never to appear overly friendly and to immediately suspect those who were. "Leavenworth," he said without blinking.

"I hear it's a fine town," Wilton replied, always quick to find something nice to say about a person or a place.

"I wouldn't know. I didn't spend much time in town."

Wilton nodded as though it made complete sense, then turned to Mel. "I know why you fainted," he said, changing the subject abruptly.

She fidgeted with her buttons again. "You do?" she asked, still trying to figure out how Kane had gotten out of prison. All sorts of images flashed through her head; Kane scaling a nine-foot concrete wall, Kane cutting through barbed wire. Or maybe he'd put a makeshift knife to a guard's throat and walked through the front doors.

Wilton faced Kane once more. "She's been listening to that skinny sister of hers."

"The model from New York?" Kane asked, remembering how often Mel had mentioned her younger sibling in her letters.

"That's the one," Wilton told him. "Blair's as skinny as a two-by-four, but she has to starve herself to stay that way. Anyhow, Blair got miffed with Mel the other day at breakfast for eating waffles. Called her pudgy."

Mel's cheeks burned. "Daddy, I'm sure Mr. Stoddard isn't interested—"

Wilton ignored her. "See, Mel can eat anything she likes, and she doesn't gain weight 'cause she works it off. Blair don't so much as lift her little finger. But Mel must've taken what her sister said to heart 'cause she hasn't eaten a decent meal in days." He faced his daughter. "I thought you had better sense than to listen to Blair."

"You're definitely not pudgy," Kane said, his eyes raking boldly over her. She was slender and healthy-looking with curves in all the right places. He was both surprised and pleased by what he saw.

Mel felt her mouth go dry as the bearded man scrutinized her as thoroughly as one might a broodmare. "Would you please step back so I can stand?" she asked, wanting desperately to put some distance between them.

"Yeah, and after you do that, you can take her somewhere to get something to eat," Wilton said.

Mel gave her father what he'd often referred to as one of *those* looks. The last time she'd given him such a look was when he'd gone to the front of the church to rededicate his life to the Lord, and his fly had been unzipped.

"Daddy, I'm sure Mr. Stoddard has better things to do with his time than take me to lunch."

"No, I don't," Kane replied. "I've got all the time in the world."

"See there?" Wilton said. "Now there's a gentleman if I ever saw one."

Mel wanted to shake her father till his teeth rattled. Couldn't he see they weren't dealing with the average citizen here? Did he not notice Kane's long hair, the bushy, ill-kept beard, and that thick piece of chain in his left ear? Had he totally overlooked Kane's filthy biker boots and grungy clothes that made him resemble an . . . an *escaped convict*, for heaven's sake?

Mel was so jolted by the thought that she was half-afraid she would faint again.

Nevertheless, she knew her father would not notice Kane's shortcomings. Wilton Abercrombie only saw goodness in people. Even when he was forced to acknowledge Blair's faults, he always took time to point out her assets as well.

"I appreciate the offer, Mr. Stoddard," Mel said at last, trying to make her voice sound natural despite a sudden attack of nerves, "but I really need to stay and clear these shelves."

Kane cupped her elbow with one hand. "Oh, but I *insist*, Miss Abercrombie," he said, his tone final and matter-of-fact. He had to talk to her. He needed a job and a place to live right away. If anybody could advise him on either, he knew Melanie Abercrombie was the one.

Mel opened her mouth to protest, but the look in his eyes stopped her cold. He flashed her a gentle but firm warning. What did he mean, he *insisted*? Here he was, a convicted criminal, serving time for robbing a convenience store and killing the clerk, and he was *insisting* she go with him? She tried to remain calm, but it was not easy. If he had *indeed* escaped, that could only mean one thing: He expected her to hide him.

Mel glanced at her father, wishing there was some way to let him know they were in danger. Her heart turned over in her chest at the thought of his getting hurt. She couldn't risk it. She would do whatever Kane Stoddard wished.

"On second thought, I'd love to go," she said, trying to sound enthusiastic. Nevertheless, her legs shook as she made her way to the door. She stepped out, spied the enormous motorcycle, and froze. "You don't expect me to ride *that*!"

Kane almost smiled at the thought of her riding his motorcycle in her frumpy clothes, her skirt flapping in the breeze like a banner. "You're right, I don't," he said.

Mel led him across the parking lot to a white late-model station wagon and opened the door.

"Mind if I toss my duffel bag in the backseat?" Kane asked.

"Suit yourself." Mel climbed into the car and fumbled through her purse for her keys. He joined her, shoving his seat back as far as it would go to accommodate his long legs. "Where do you want to eat?" she asked as she started the car and pulled out onto the narrow two-lane highway.

"That's up to you," Kane told her, figuring shet would know where the best food was served. "Just as long as there are not a lot of people," he added, remembering the long lines in prison, being jammed elbow to elbow at the dining table with men who didn't practice good hygiene on a regular basis. "Crowds make me uncomfortable."

Mel wasn't surprised. If he was hiding out, it made

sense he'd want to keep a low profile. "There's a house not far from here. It belongs to my best friend and her husband. They're on vacation in Florida. I have the key." Mel said a silent apology to her friend who'd asked her to water her plants while she was away. But where else could she take him? She had to convince Kane that she was willing to help him. Once he trusted her, she could go for help. "You have to promise not to bother anything."

Kane didn't quite know how to respond to her offer of free lodging when all he'd expected was the name of a place where he could rent something cheap. "Thanks," he said, thinking he should at least show his appreciation, although doing so didn't come easy to him. Not that he was used to folks going out of their way for him. He'd learned at an early age that if he wanted something, he had to *take* it. He couldn't help but wonder why Melanie Abercrombie was so eager to help. Was she doing it out of the goodness of her heart, or did she have an ulterior motive? Most folks, if you looked closely enough, never did anything unless it benefited them in some way. At least that's what he'd discovered. "I won't mess with their stuff," he added.

Mel turned onto a dirt road and pulled in front of a frame house with a narrow porch. "This is it," she said, as she cut the engine.

Kane glanced across the seat at the woman driving and found himself wondering about her, not for the first time. She'd told him very little about herself over the past months, writing mostly about her family and the town in which she'd grown up. Now he was curious. Was there a man in her life? Why did she try to hide her femininity and good looks with unattractive clothes and ugly glasses? And why was she so nervous? Was she sorry he'd come? He glanced at the house, then back at her. "I thought we were going to a restaurant first."

She snapped her head around. "How can you *possibly* think of eating at a time like this?"

He could see that she was truly upset. "I wasn't asking for myself," he said. "I promised your father I'd see that you ate."

Mel had had enough of his games. Here he was, expecting her to risk her neck by hiding him from the police, and he was pretending to be concerned about whether or not she was fed. "How kind of you," she blurted, her voice edged with sarcasm. "I suppose you'd feel guilty shooting me on an empty stomach." The car was suddenly silent. Mel regretted her words the moment she said them, but it was too late to take them back. Instead, she gazed out the window wordlessly, afraid to move or even breathe.

Kane wondered if he'd heard her correctly. "What did you say?"

Tears welled up in her eyes, and Mel blinked furiously to hold them back. She would not give him the satisfaction of knowing how frightened she was.

"Don't pretend you aren't considering it," she said. "After all, I can identify you."

He stared back at her for a full minute. "Lady, I don't have the first clue what you're talking about. I've never shot anybody in my life. Why would I want to start with you?"

One fat tear fell from her eye and rolled down her cheek. "You don't really expect me to believe that. I know why you were imprisoned. The warden told me."

"You talked to the warden at Leavenworth?"

She hitched her chin high. "That's right. After I wrote several letters to you and got no answer, I called to make sure you had received them. The warden told me about the man you shot."

"And you believed him?" When she didn't answer, Kane decided she had believed what she'd been told. He clenched his fists in his lap. He could feel his anger mounting, intensifying with each breath he took. Wasn't that *always* the way? People automatically believed the worst about him. Just as the jury had believed the worst and convicted him of cold-blooded murder.

"So why'd you keep writing?" he asked. "If you thought I was such a lost cause." He knew there were women who wrote to convicts out of sheer loneliness. Hell, some women went so far as to marry them, although he didn't figure it was much of a life. He thought it was selfish for a prisoner to encourage such a relationship, no matter how lonely he was. Which is why, no matter how much he'd enjoyed and looked forward to Melanie Abercrombie's letters, he'd refused to take part in the correspondence and make her feel obligated.

"I was only trying to help you," Mel said.

"Help me what?" When she refused to answer, he gripped her arm. "Look at me when I talk to you."

Mel flinched. His fingers were warm and strong. She looked at him. His black eyes glittered dangerously. She wondered if prison had hardened him, or if he'd been that way before going in. She wondered if he would hurt her. "What do you want me to say?"

"I want to know why you kept writing when I never so much as answered the first letter. Did it turn you on to write to a convicted killer?"

"That's sick."

"Yeah, but it's true, isn't it? You got all hot and bothered over it, didn't you?"

"How come it's so important for you to know *why* I did it?"

"Because," was all he said. He was tempted to tell her. It was important because she had literally changed the direction of his life. She had done what youth-detention centers and the penal system had failed to do. Through her letters, he had discovered an entirely different way of life. Now he wanted to know why she had bothered when everyone else had given up. Had she simply been trying to bring her quota of souls to salvation, or had she genuinely cared about the embittered man sitting in Leavenworth Prison?

Mel turned away once more. How could she explain her reasons to a man she barely knew? He would never understand what it was like living in the same house all your life, in the same small town where everybody knew everybody else and nothing much ever happened to break the monotony. Even her relationship with Harper Beckwood wasn't likely to bloom into the passionate sort of love that conjured up sonnets and love songs. All she had was her little flower shop, and that, as much as she loved it, wasn't enough. Writing to Kane had filled her with a sense of accomplishment. Perhaps she could make a difference in *his* life, she'd told herself.

"I just wanted to help," she repeated at last. "I thought—"

"What did you think?" he interrupted. "That you could save my sorry soul?" He laughed, but the sound was totally without mirth. "What makes you think I have one?"

"Everyone has a soul," she replied.

"It's not my soul that ails me at the moment," he said, his tone deadly.

Mel's head snapped up, and their gazes collided. There was a restless sort of energy about him. The expression on his face reminded her of gathering storm clouds. He raised his hand to her cheek. She flinched.

"I only want to touch you," he said. His voice, though quiet, possessed an ominous quality.

Mel sat riveted as he explored her face with warm fingertips. He stroked her cheek, then traced the outline of her mouth and jaw. Her cheeks grew pink under the heat of his stare. She held her breath as he slid his fingers down her throat.

Kane noted the tense lines on her face, the rapid rise and fall of her breasts. "It's been three years since I've touched a woman," he said. "Salvation is not exactly what I'm looking for."

His look was so intense, it sent a tremor through her. She watched his grim-faced expression turn to desire. He exuded danger. "Please don't," she said, her voice a mere whisper.

The shudder that passed through her did not go unnoticed by Kane. He snatched his hand away. What was she thinking? "I'm sorry you find me so repulsive," he said, clenching his teeth as anger surged through him. "Or maybe you think you're too damn good for me." He reached for the door handle, feeling as though he would tear it off if he didn't get out of the car soon. He was both embarrassed and disappointed. This was not the same woman who'd encouraged him to hope and dream again, reminding him over and over that the past did not equal the future. He climbed out and reached for his duffel bag. His black eyes blazed with fire as he regarded her, huddled against her side of the car as though she couldn't bear for him to touch her, even by accident.

"You're one self-righteous woman, you know that? I was a fool to think you'd be happy over my release, but your letters were so convincing. I guess that makes you a phony as well, doesn't it?" He didn't give her a chance to answer. Instead, he backed away and slammed the door so hard, it rocked the car.

Feeling very fragile after the way Kane had talked to her, Mel watched him stalk away, his duffel bag thrown over one broad shoulder. Her fear ebbed somewhat once she realized he wasn't going to hurt her after all. She sat there, blank, amazed, and terribly shaken. What the heck did he mean, he'd been released?

Hands trembling, she started the car and put it in reverse. She wanted to escape but couldn't. Something more powerful than common sense drove her.

She went after him.

She found Kane walking along the road, his strides long and purposeful, headed for the interstate. From there he could go in a number of directions.

Suddenly, she knew she had to stop him. At least until she learned the circumstances of his release. She slowed the car and rolled down the window. Kane glanced up, saw it was her, and kept walking.

"Mr. Stoddard, wait, I have to talk to you," she called out through the open window. He ignored her. She persisted. "What do you mean you were released?"

Kane paused and looked at the sky as though trying to decide whether to deal with her or tell her to go straight to hell. "They found the man who committed the crime."

"You mean you were serving time for a crime you didn't commit?"

"Something like that, yeah." He turned and started down the road again. The sooner he got away from Hooterville and Miss Melanie Abercrombie, the better.

Mel touched the accelerator. The car rolled forward. She leaned across the passenger seat once more and called out to him through the window. "Why didn't you tell me?"

He kept on walking. "Would you have believed me?" He obviously didn't expect an answer, because he didn't so much as look at her.

Mel continued to roll along the road beside him. "So they let you out because they found the real killer?"

"How else would I have gotten out?"

"Well, you could have escaped."

He stopped dead in his tracks and gave her a funny look. "Is that what you thought?"

She was embarrassed to have to admit it. "It crossed my mind."

"So that's why you were acting weird. Do you

think I'd be crazy enough to pull a stunt like that?"
He frowned in exasperation and walked away. "I gotta
go. I've wasted enough time."

"No, wait!" But he was already moving away from
the car. Mel followed, pulling off the road onto the
shoulder so she would not impede other motorists.
She tried to ignore the looks she received as she
followed directly behind the man, yelling out her
window to him. "Kane, I'm sorry for what I thought,"
she said, deciding she could drop the formality. "I had
no idea you were innocent or that they'd released you.
I mean, what was I *supposed* to think? Here you are
serving life without parole, and you show up out of
the blue. What would *you* think?"

He didn't answer, didn't even bother to slow
down.

"I'm sorry I let you down. You have a right to be
angry with me. I'd like to make it up to you."

He stopped dead in his tracks and turned. "What
did you have in mind?" he called back.

Mel was not prepared for his sudden halt or the
blatant innuendo. She slammed on the brakes, spit-
ting gravel in all directions. The car careened, and
she tried to right it, but it was too late. The next
thing she knew, she was sliding toward the ditch.

THREE

The car seemed to take forever to reach the bottom
of the ravine, although in reality it happened in a
matter of seconds. Held in place by her seat belt, Mel
closed her eyes, covered her head with her hands,
and prepared to die. When, at last, the car came to
a jaw-jolting halt at the bottom, she opened her eyes
and found her headlights pointed straight down.

Having watched the whole thing in disbelief, Kane
dropped his duffel bag and hurried down the steep
ditch. Anxiety knotted his gut when he realized it was
probably his fault she'd gone down. He found her
leaning against the steering wheel. "Are you okay?"
he yelled. He banged on the window to make sure
she heard him.

Trembling from head to foot, Mel raised up
and glared at the man who somehow managed
to look compassionate at the moment, despite the

beard. Nevertheless, angry tears stung her eyes. "Go away!" she said. "Just go away and leave me alone."

Kane was too relieved to be angry. "Why are you mad at me?" he asked. "I haven't done anything." When she didn't respond, he went on. "Come on, now, open the door. I need to make sure you're okay."

Mel was more humiliated than anything. She rolled down her window. "Look, I'm perfectly fine. I just want to be left alone."

"I'm not leaving you at the bottom of some damn ditch," he stated flatly.

Her humiliation quickly turned to annoyance. "Must you swear?"

"Lady, you would drive a preacher to cussing," he said. "You either come on out of there, or I'll haul your fanny out personally."

"You wouldn't dare."

"Try me."

Mel nibbled her bottom lip as she regarded him. He looked like the Devil himself standing there, that coarse black beard hiding his face and making her wonder what lay beneath. "Why do you want me out so badly?" she asked.

Kane sighed heavily. Three years of prison had made him forget what it was like dealing with the opposite sex. Had women always been this stubborn, or had he suddenly met up with the queen of pigheads? "We need to call a tow truck," he said, mustering as much patience as he could.

Mel knew he was right. She couldn't leave her car at the bottom of the ravine forever, and the only way she was going to get it out was to have it towed. Still, she would have preferred going it alone. She had done nothing but make a fool of herself since Kane Stoddard hit town.

Kane was growing more impatient than ever with her silence. Women! Who could figure them? Certainly not a man who'd spent three years of his life surrounded by men. It would serve her right if he left her sitting there. But he couldn't. Whether she suspected it or not, her letters had given him a reason to get out of bed in the morning in a place where death had been preferable. He decided it was time to try another approach. After all, she was a lady.

Kane leaned closer to the window, propping his hands against the door, giving her a smile that had, in the past, charmed his share of females. Had he known there was this much trouble waiting in Hardeeville, he would have run as fast as he could in the opposite direction.

"I'm sorry we got off to a bad start, Miss Abercrombie," he said, using a tone that was meant to inspire confidence, "and I'm sorry for the things I said. I don't feel good about leaving you out in the middle of nowhere. At least let me escort you to the nearest phone so you can call for help. After that, I'll be on my way."

She looked surprised. "And go where?"

It was working. "You let me worry about that."

Heaving one last sigh, Mel grabbed her purse from the front seat of the car, climbed out, and followed him up the ravine, allowing him to assist her.

"Which way to the nearest phone?" he asked when they reached the top.

Mel motioned in the direction of the house they'd just left. "My friend wouldn't mind me using hers."

Kane picked up his duffel bag, and they started for the house that was no more than an eighth of a mile away. They walked in silence, neither knowing what to say. Mel was careful not to brush his hand as they went, but she couldn't help but notice the arm next to her: bare, slightly muscular, and feathered with silky black hair. Very nice as arms went.

Once at the house, Mel unlocked the front door and went in. "It's okay for you to come in too," she said. She waited for him to follow, then went straight for the phone.

Kane stood inside the door and waited while Mel looked up a phone number in a thin directory and dialed. He took a moment to study his surroundings while she talked to the person on the other end of the line. The living room was small and filled with various houseplants. A television set along one wall held an assortment of picture frames, and the mantel over the fireplace housed what looked like an antique bottle collection.

He took it all in with relish, trying to remember the last time he'd been in a private home. Nevertheless, he felt uncomfortable. Not only did he not know the owners, he'd just served time in a penitentiary. If the couple ever learned he was there, they'd start looking high and low to find something missing. Of course, before his incarceration he wouldn't have thought twice about taking anything. Habit alone made him wonder about the value of the TV set and bottle collection. He took a step back, positioning himself closer to the door. He looked up when Mel hung up the phone.

"Sure is different from what I'm used to," he said, smiling self-consciously.

Mel felt a sudden, unexpected wave of tenderness for him and wondered what his life had been like behind bars. "Yes, I'm sure it is. But just think, before long you'll have your own place."

"It can't happen fast enough for me," he said, wondering if she had any idea how long he'd dreamed of it. He would never again have to share a toilet or try to sleep while his bunk mate snored. "Did you find a tow truck?" he asked, giving none of his thoughts away.

She nodded. She wasn't the least bit afraid now that she knew the truth about him. "There's only one place in town with a tow truck. It's being used right now, but they should have it here in about an hour." She paused. "Would you like a cup of coffee? There's no need to hurry, and I know my friend wouldn't mind."

Kane shrugged. He wasn't much of a coffee drinker, but he liked the idea of spending a few minutes more in the cozy surroundings. Funny, what prison made you appreciate. "Yeah, sure," he said, following her into a spotless compact kitchen.

It didn't take Mel long to find what she needed to make coffee. She had spent many evenings sipping coffee in this same kitchen after choir practice while she and her friend Camille talked long into the night about all sorts of things. She motioned for Kane to sit at the small table as she scooped coffee grounds from one of the canisters into the percolator. She plugged it in, then turned when she heard Kane chuckling from his place at the table.

He looked less menacing when he smiled. His teeth were a brilliant white against the beard. "What's so funny?" she asked.

"You thinking I'd escaped."

She chuckled as well. "What was I supposed to think? You didn't tell me you were getting out. You never so much as answered any of my letters."

"I'm not much for writing letters."

"Obviously."

"So why'd you keep writing?" he asked, for the second time in less than an hour.

She regarded him. "I hoped it would make a difference."

"It did." She arched one brow at him, and he knew she wanted him to elaborate. He decided it was time to change the subject. "What do you think my chances are of finding a job around here?" he said instead, watching her closely for a reaction.

Mel didn't try to mask her surprise. "You're thinking of staying in Hardeeville?"

"Would it bother you?"

"No, of course not. I'm just surprised, that's all. I wouldn't have thought small-town life would appeal to someone like you."

"Someone like me?" He tensed. "You mean an ex-con?"

She blushed. "That's not what I meant at all. It's just, well, Hardeeville is small, and there's not a lot to do. My sister, Blair, just hates it here. The only time she comes around is when her life falls apart in New York."

"Is that why she's home now?"

Mel realized she may have said too much. "She's not happy with the way her career is going," she said, deciding the small confidence wouldn't hurt her sister.

"I thought her modeling was going well."

Mel reached into a cabinet for two coffee cups. "She wants to be an actress. That's why she went to New York in the first place. She's had a couple of small parts here and there, but nothing significant." Mel didn't think it would be fair to Blair to say anything more. Although Blair's modeling career had supported her well these past few years and allowed her to rub elbows with the rich and famous, she had never hit it big. Now, at twenty-eight, she was beginning to panic. With younger faces appearing on the covers of magazines, Blair wanted desperately to move on to something bigger and better.

"What do you take in your coffee?" Mel asked, changing the subject.

"I've been drinking it black for the past three years," he said, pleased he had a choice now. "Maybe I should try something different."

She put cream and sugar in the cup, stirred, then handed it to him.

He took a sip and was tempted to close his eyes from the sheer pleasure of it. It was odd what people took for granted. Until prison, he'd never appreciated a damn thing. Now he was grateful for *everything*. "I could get used to this."

Mel smiled as she joined him at the table. It was fun watching his reaction to new things. It also made him appear almost vulnerable, although she was certain he would deny it as long as he had breath in his body. "So, what kind of work are you looking for?"

"I worked in the print shop at Leavenworth, so I figured I could start interviewing in that area."

"We only have one print shop in Hardeeville, but I know the owners personally. I could call them—"

"I'd rather you didn't," Kane interrupted, deciding she had already done enough. He didn't want to be indebted to her or anyone else. When she looked surprised, he went on. "I'd prefer doing it on my own."

"I understand."

He drained his coffee cup and set it down. "I could really use your advice on a place to live, though," he said. "Preferably something cheap."

"There's Yardley's Boardinghouse in town," Mel told him. "Nothing fancy, but it's clean and inexpensive. You might have to share a bathroom."

Kane frowned. Okay, so maybe he had to share a toilet for a little while longer. It wasn't forever. "Some things never change," he muttered. He glanced at the clock on the wall. "We'd best get back to your car."

Mel rinsed out the coffeepot and their cups and set them on a towel to dry. There was something strangely intimate in the act. She checked a couple of potted plants near the window she had watered two days before to make sure the dirt was still moist. Once she was convinced everything was okay, she followed Kane out the front door and locked it.

"You ever had your own place?" he asked as they started down the road, him with his duffel bag on one shoulder.

She shook her head, glad the walk back wasn't as tense as the one coming up. "I've always lived with my father."

"Where's your mother?"

Mel glanced at him, then straight ahead. She didn't often talk about the woman who'd given birth to her. "My mother left when Blair and I were little."

"That must've been tough."

"At first. We hardly ever think about it now."

"She's never tried to contact you?"

His questions made Mel uneasy and touched on painful decisions she had made within the last year concerning her mother. "My mother was not happy living with us. She hated Hardeeville as much as Blair does. If I never see her again, it'll be too soon as far as I'm concerned. Oh, look, there's the tow truck now," she said, picking up her pace. She was thankful for the diversion. Thinking about her mother always left a bad taste in her mouth.

The air had cooled considerably by the time Mel parked in front of her house with Kane behind on his motorcycle. Once her car had been pulled from the ditch, he'd suggested they take it to a self-service car wash and clean it up. Luckily, the car hadn't been damaged. She'd been so thankful that she'd insisted Kane come to dinner.

Mel noticed him studying everything closely as he parked his bike and climbed off. She was glad she and her father had managed to keep up with the yard work. The boxwood hedges were neatly trimmed, the sweet peas already blooming, creating a myriad of colors. A large Martha Washington geranium hung on the front porch.

"Well, here we are," she announced once she'd climbed out of the car.

"It looks like a Norman Rockwell painting," Kane said, joining her on the flagstone walk that led to the small farmhouse.

"You're familiar with Norman Rockwell's work?"

He fixed her with a cool look. "Yeah, when I'm not stealing wallets and cutting throats, I like to study his stuff."

She could feel the color staining her cheeks. "That's not what I meant."

"Isn't it?" She obviously considered him a dullard and a hood. And maybe he had been before prison, but he had utilized his time well. He'd made the weeks and months count.

"Kane—" She paused and met his black-eyed gaze. "I can't be your friend if you're going to misunderstand everything I say."

He studied her intently. Had he misread her? All his life he'd been treated like trash. He'd come to expect it. What made her different? He wanted to ask, but he didn't feel he knew her well enough.

"I've never met a woman who blushed as easily as you do," he said instead, changing the subject because it seemed like a safer topic.

Whatever Mel may have expected him to say, that was not it. "Yes, well, I've never met a man who was so quick-tempered." She smiled, hoping to ease the tension between them. "Let's go in. I don't know about you, but I'm as hungry as a bear."

Duffel bag propped on one shoulder, Kane followed her up the short walk to the front porch as a fat tabby cat awoke from his late afternoon nap and raced toward Mel, rubbing against her legs as she climbed the steps. Mel laughed, stopping long enough to pet him affectionately. "This is Hercules," she said, introducing Kane to the animal. "Someone found him in a Dumpster, half-starved, when he was only a couple of days old. Dad and I had to feed him with an eyedropper to keep him alive."

Kane leaned over and scratched the cat behind one ear. He purred in response. "He doesn't look as if he's missed any meals since."

Mel was just about to respond when the front door was thrown open by a blonde who could only be described as drop-dead gorgeous.

"What took you so long?" she demanded. "Daddy wants his supper." Her eyes drifted to Kane, then opened wide in surprise. She folded her arms in front of her and stepped back as though suddenly feeling the need to defend herself. "Who is *that*?"

Kane shifted from one foot to the other. He suddenly felt like a circus freak under the woman's appalled gaze. He disliked her instantly.

"This is Kane Stoddard," Mel said, embarrassed by her sister's rudeness. Blair didn't have a diplomatic bone in her body. "He's new in town." She paused briefly, noting the way Kane stared in return. She wasn't surprised. Most men couldn't take their eyes off her sister. "Kane, this is Blair."

Kane started to offer his hand, then thought better of it. "Nice to meet you," he said, as he followed Mel inside, with Blair watching him as though she expected him to whip out a pistol and start shooting.

"Why is he here?" Blair asked.

Kane tensed. The woman was passing judgment on him, and she didn't know the first thing about him. All his insecurities, and his anger, sprang to life. From somewhere in his head a voice mocked him. He was Harmon Stoddard's kid. He'd never amount to anything.

Mel saw Kane's look and knew she had to move fast. As irritated as she was with Blair's behavior, though, she couldn't place all the blame on her. Kane didn't look like the sort of man you'd bring to dinner. "I accidentally ran my car off Roper's Road," she told her sister. "Kane waited with me until a tow truck came. I invited him for dinner. Have you put the pork chops in the oven yet?" she asked, hoping to take the focus off Kane.

Blair gave her a look that suggested she had obviously lost her marbles at the bottom of the ditch as well. "You know I can't cook."

"I tried to tell her how to do it," Wilton Abercrombie said, coming into the room, "but she insisted on waiting for you."

Mel sometimes wondered how her family had become so helpless. "Daddy, you remember Kane Stoddard," she said, repeating the story of how she'd run off the road.

"You're staying for dinner, right?" Wilton said, as soon as he was convinced his daughter was unharmed.

"Of course he is," Mel told him. She looked at Kane. "I know you're anxious to get cleaned up," she said, hoping he would take the hint without being offended. "Daddy, if you'll show Kane where he can take a shower, I'll get dinner on. Oh, and Kane, I'll toss your clothes in the washer if you like."

Mel hurried into the kitchen and to the refrigerator, where the package of pork chops was still wrapped as they'd come from the store. She turned around and bumped into Blair who was right behind her. "Would you please make a salad?" she asked her sister, knowing it was the one thing she could prepare.

"Just *what* do you think you're doing?" Blair hissed.

Mel reached beneath the oven for the broiler pan. "What do you mean?" she said, being deliberately obtuse. She did not feel like getting into a heated discussion about Kane at the moment. Especially with him just down the hall.

"What is that man doing in this house!"

"I told you. I invited him for dinner."

"Oh, really, Mel!" Blair let out an exasperated sigh. "It's bad enough you and Daddy pick up every stray animal you find. Must you bring homeless victims into our house as well? Can't you see that man is nasty?"

Mel gave her sister a long, hard look. "His clothes are grungy," she said, "but that's only because he's been on the road for several days." She tore open the package of meat. "I know he looks rough, Blair. I was shocked at first. But once you get to know him—"

Blair drew back as though she'd been slapped. "I don't *plan* to get to know him. The man looks as if he belongs behind bars."

Wilton Abercrombie stepped into the room. "Chill out, Blair." He chuckled at his own choice of words.

"Daddy, I can't believe you let Mel bring that awful man here."

Wilton made his way to the refrigerator, where he pulled out a pitcher of tea. "This is Mel's house too. I reckon she can bring anyone she likes into it." He glanced at his oldest daughter. "I've invited him to spend the night."

All the color drained from Blair's face. "My God, you're as bad as she is."

"Where's he going to sleep?" Mel asked her father, trying to ignore her sister's theatrics. It was times like this that she couldn't help but wonder why Blair hadn't made it big as an actress.

"He can sleep in the attic," Wilton said. "There's even a roll-away bed stored up there as I remember."

"I don't know, it gets awfully hot in the attic," Mel told him, then decided after what Kane was used to, it might seem like the Hilton.

"I'll carry that big fan up from the garage. That thing would cool the Sahara Desert."

Blair shook her head sadly. "You are *both* out of your minds, you know that?"

"That's enough," Wilton told her. "You know how I feel about helping the less fortunate."

"Yes, Daddy, I know how you feel," she said. "But it's *not* your Christian duty to invite hoodlums into our home."

Blair was still trying to drag Mel to her senses as they put the finishing touches on dinner. "Okay, have it your way," she said. "But don't expect *me* to be nice to the man."

The pork chops had been baked to a golden brown, the potatoes mashed until there wasn't a lump to be found, and the biscuits were just waiting to be dipped in the gravy Mel had prepared. There were field peas with fresh chopped onion and stewed tomatoes, all of which had come from Mel's vegetable garden the previous year. She wanted everything to be perfect. Not only did they have a house guest, they had a man who hadn't eaten a home-cooked meal in three years.

So where *was* Kane? He'd been holed up in the bathroom for more than an hour.

Mel cleared her throat. "Daddy, I think you better knock on the bathroom door again."

"I've already knocked twice."

"He's probably not even in there," Blair said. "Most likely, he's stolen our prescription drugs and climbed out the bathroom window." She picked up her fork and started eating her salad, announcing to her family that she was tired of waiting.

The sound of the bathroom door opening down the hall cut off any reply Mel might have made. She sat completely still as approaching footsteps sounded in the hall. With her back to the door, Mel didn't see Kane when he first entered the room. All she saw was the shocked expression on Blair's face, followed by the clatter of her fork when she dropped it. The noise made Mel jump. She swung her head around and gasped out loud at the sight of Kane Stoddard.

The grizzled beard was gone, leaving behind a face so devastatingly handsome that Mel half feared she might faint again.

FOUR

Kane stood there for a full minute, feeling very self-conscious with the looks he was receiving. "Is something wrong?" he asked.

Mel finally found her tongue. "Please forgive us for staring, Kane. It's just, you look so different, we barely recognize you without the beard." The transformation was like nothing she'd ever witnessed. He had a strong sensual face, a square jaw that suggested either stubbornness or determination. His hair, still wet from his shower, was pulled back with a rubber band.

Kane rubbed his cheek. "I've been wanting to shave it off for some time," he confessed. "It was beginning to itch."

"Please join us," Wilton said, obviously in a hurry to start eating. "Mel has really outdone herself this time."

Kane took the vacant chair. "Everything looks great," he said, feeling out of place at the old-fashioned pine table.

"Would you like some mashed potatoes, Kane?" Blair asked in a voice that literally dripped with honey. Three pairs of eyes followed that voice and found a radiant Blair at the other end. The woman who'd sworn only a moment before that she wouldn't even speak to him had gone through some sort of transformation herself.

Mel noted the look of surprise on Kane's face as he accepted the bowl of mashed potatoes from her sister. Her heart sank as she watched Blair turn on her charm. How many times had she witnessed that charm at work? A man didn't stand a chance.

"Aren't you having any?" he asked.

Blair smiled until her dimples showed. "Just salad for me, I'm afraid."

"Blair only eats rabbit food," Wilton said, stabbing a pork chop with his fork. He winked at Kane. "She can't afford to have any meat on her bones."

"I've already told you, Daddy. A camera adds ten to fifteen pounds to a body. I can't hide the extra weight under big T-shirts the way Mel does."

Mel felt her cheeks burn at the remark, but she was determined not to let it bother her. She knew Blair put more emphasis on food than was normal, and she supposed it had to do with the fact that weight was such an issue in her line of work. Nevertheless, while Blair pretended to starve herself, Mel knew she often slipped into the kitchen at night and gorged on leftovers and junk food. Sad as it was, it was not something she felt she could discuss with her sister.

"I like being comfortable," Mel said, offering a shrug of indifference. "I guess it's lucky for me that baggy shirts are in style."

"You don't need to change a thing about yourself," Kane blurted out, wondering why Mel didn't defend herself to her sister when he would have been more than happy to tell the skinny blonde where she could get off. "I like a healthy woman."

Mel's mouth dropped open at the comment, and she almost dropped the bowl of mashed potatoes he handed her. She raised her eyes to his and found him watching her, assessing her frankly and offering his approval in one look. "Thank you," she managed, at the same time wondering if he was only feeling sorry for her. She had learned a long time ago not to take Blair's remarks seriously.

Blair poured a liberal amount of dressing on her salad. "Yes, well, that's our Mel for you. She's always been healthy as a horse. So tell me, Kane, what brings you to Hardeeville?"

"I heard it was a nice place to live," he said, uncomfortable with the attention he was getting from the woman. Blair hadn't stopped staring and fluttering her lashes since he'd walked into the room. It was embarrassing, especially in front of Mel, who had more sense than to waste her time with such silliness. He'd felt more comfortable when Blair hadn't liked him. "I'm looking to find a job and settle down," he added.

"I understand you're from Leavenworth," Blair said. "What were you doing there?"

Kane glanced at Mel, then back at the blonde. It was a rotten thing to do, but he couldn't help himself. "I was serving time for murder."

Blair came close to dropping her salad fork again. Wilton almost choked on his pork chop. Mel spilled her iced tea down the front of her blouse, then tried to mop it with her napkin.

Kane shot her an apologetic look. "I'm sorry. I just don't think it's fair to lie. I figure they'll find out sooner or later."

The room went completely quiet. From his end of the table Wilton shifted uneasily in his chair. He regarded Mel. "Is that true?"

She glanced at Kane, then back to her father. "Yes, Daddy. I've been writing to Kane at Leavenworth Prison for the past year." She explained how she'd gotten his name from Reverend Potts.

Wilton returned his attention to Kane. "If you were convicted of murder, how come you're out?"

"They found the real killer."

"You're saying you didn't do it?"

Kane met his gaze. "That's right."

Wilton visibly relaxed. "Then I'm sorry you had to serve time for a crime you didn't commit. If there's something we can do to help, you let me know."

Kane was both surprised and touched. "I appreciate it, Mr. Abercrombie."

"Call me Wilton."

They proceeded with their meal. Blair looked from one to the other, then back to her father. The smile was gone. "That's it?" she asked. "You're just going to take his word for it—a complete stranger's—that he didn't do it?" The change in her was as dramatic as before.

Once again, Kane's jaw tensed, and his face hardened as though it had been carved from stone.

Mel held her breath.

Wilton chewed his food slowly, then swallowed, as though unaware of the tension in the room. "He's out of prison, ain't he? I reckon that says something."

"He could have escaped, for all we know."

Mel's blood chilled at the dangerous look on Kane's face. But then, why shouldn't he be angry; he'd done nothing but defend himself since he'd hit town.

Blair looked at Kane. It was obvious she didn't think he was good enough to sit at the same table with her. "How long were you in?"

"Three years."

"Oh, my Lord!" Blair shot Mel a terrified look. "You brought a *hardened* criminal into our house?"

"That's enough, Blair," Wilton said. "Mr. Stoddard is our guest. I don't know how ya'll treat company in New York City, but here we treat them with respect. Now I'd like to eat my meal in peace, if you don't mind."

"But, Daddy—" Wilton gave her a look that shut her up.

Kane relaxed his shoulders.

Mel sighed her relief.

Blair was sullen throughout the rest of the meal, and Mel was thankful when she finally excused herself and went to her room. Wilton apologized for his younger daughter's behavior.

"Blair's unhappy with her life right now," he told Kane. "That's why she's striking out at people. Once she gets her problems worked out, she'll be okay."

Kane offered him a bleak, tight-lipped smile. "Maybe it's best if I don't stay."

"Nonsense. This is my house and I insist." Wilton got up from the table and carried his plate to the sink.

"Don't worry about helping in the kitchen tonight, Daddy," Mel told him, as it was his habit to assist in the cleanup since she always did the cooking. "I'll get it."

Wilton smiled and patted her on the shoulder. He looked more tired than usual. "You'll see that Kane is settled in?" he asked.

"Of course." She watched him go, then turned

her gaze to Kane. She found him watching her. The tight-faced expression was gone, replaced now with a curious half-smile that was as unexpected as snow in July. She wondered if he had any idea how good-looking he was when he wasn't scowling. She was a nervous wreck just sitting in the same room with him.

"What is it?" she asked, when he continued to stare.

"You and your dad are very close."

"Nothing wrong with that, is there?" she said, hearing the censure in his voice.

He shrugged. "Not as long as you're happy." He paused. "You know, in all the time you wrote, you never once mentioned having a man in your life."

Mel tensed. "I don't usually discuss my personal life with strangers," she said, "but since you asked, I'll tell you I've been seeing someone for the past six months. We're sort of going together." She figured that would explain why she had dated only one man in six months. It was better than having to admit no one else had asked her out.

He arched one brow questioningly. "How do you *sort of* go with someone?"

"Well, to make a long story short, his wife died last year and left him with a young daughter to raise. We don't want to rush into anything for her sake. She might think I'm trying to take her mother's place." She paused. "Amy and I are very close, though. I help her with her homework and take her shopping when she needs clothes. You couldn't ask for a sweeter eight-year-old."

"What about her father?" Kane asked, feeling a bit protective of the woman who seemed to do so much for other people. "Shouldn't you be singing his praises as well?"

"Harper Beckwood is a wonderful man," she said defensively. "He has a good job with the Board of Education, and he's active in the church. Folks just love him."

"Sounds like a regular saint to me," Kane said, his voice edged with sarcasm. Hearing how the man had become so successful only reminded him of how he'd screwed up his own life.

Mel noticed the edge in his voice and wondered if she had offended him. He was as unpredictable as spring weather. Perhaps she shouldn't have bragged on Harper so. "You've got a lot going for you, too, Kane."

He gazed at her steadily. He knew she was only trying to be nice, but it irked the hell out of him that she'd been able to read his emotions so easily.

"Tell you what," he said, wanting to change the subject. "Why don't we see how fast we can get this place cleaned up." He motioned to the table full of dirty dishes. "You wash, and I'll dry."

Dusk had fallen by the time Mel led Kane out back to a large pen holding a half-dozen dogs of various shapes and sizes. Several makeshift doghouses stood at one end, obviously built to offer protection against the rain and cold. As they approached the pen, the dogs started yapping wildly. "Do they belong to you?" Kane asked, figuring if they did, then Mel must be one helluva dog lover.

She chuckled. "Good Lord no." She paused beside a rickety gate, unlatched it, and slid through cautiously so none of the animals could escape. She was suddenly overtaken by a group of tail-wagging mongrels, and she had to pause to pet and speak to each one. Fortunately, she had changed into old jeans.

"I volunteer for the local pet-adoption program," she said, motioning for him to hand her the bag of food he'd carried out for her. She began filling bowls, playing referee as she did so to ensure that no dog went without. They quieted as they began to eat. "If someone finds a stray, they call me. I keep the animals until they're adopted."

"Sounds expensive," Kane said.

"Our local vet helps with the cost, and folks are real good about leaving donations when they take an animal."

Kane chuckled as a frisky black puppy ate from a bowl in which his two front feet were buried under the food. Mel followed his gaze and grinned. "That's

Little Bit," she said. "His mother was killed on the highway when he and his sisters were only ten days old. I found homes for the girls. It won't be long before he has one. Everybody loves puppies. It's the older animals I have trouble placing."

Kane couldn't help but wonder how she managed to keep up with all her responsibilities. It was obvious her family depended on her for everything. Could that be the reason she'd never married? "Hand me those two buckets," he said, pointing toward the pails that provided drinking water for the dogs. "I'll fill them up."

She did, then took a moment to clean the cage as best she could. Kane returned with the buckets and let himself in through the gate. Several of the dogs stopped eating and watched him to see if the new face was a friendly one. He knelt down on his haunches and spoke to the animals softly, surprising Mel with a side of him she hadn't seen before. His voice inspired trust. It was strong but gently coaxing. Comforting. By the time Mel finished cleaning the cage, he had won her over as well as the dogs.

"Is that the last of the chores?" Kane asked, having derived a great deal of satisfaction from the simple tasks. In prison he had volunteered for any job he could.

"Not quite," she said, smiling in a way that suggested she'd saved the best for last. "We still have to slop the hog."

"You're kidding, right?"

Kane stared down at the large Yorkshire boar who'd started snorting and slobbering the minute Mel appeared with the feed bucket. She poured the contents into the trough.

"Meet Pork Chop," Mel said, leaning over the fence and scratching the hog behind his ear. "We raised him from a baby. Each year, Daddy threatens to have him made into sausage, but he doesn't have the heart."

"So this is why you save your leftovers," Kane said, remembering how she'd refused to throw anything away when they were cleaning the kitchen. "You got any more animals I should know about?"

"We got rid of what few cows we had because there was no time to care for them. We *do* have a goat in the pasture named General Lee. He jumps out now and then and chews the towels on the clothesline."

Kane gazed at her for a long moment, appreciating the fact that she'd changed out of her librarian clothes. A soft breeze fanned his cheek, carrying with it the scent of roses. "You're lucky to have such a nice place," he said, thinking of the dumps he'd lived in as a child. "Don't ever take it for granted."

Mel was surprised by his remark. It was ironic that he should make that comment when she had spent the past couple of years wondering if this was all there was to life. Of course, there was Harper and Amy. Even though she and Harper weren't passionately in love, she looked forward to having her own family one day. "Yes, I suppose I am lucky," she said, then wondered why she still yearned for something more.

It was almost nine o'clock by the time Mel led Kane up a short flight of stairs to the attic, carrying fresh sheets in her arms. The room was small and literally crammed with boxes and old furniture. A roll-away bed stood along one wall, next to it a large fan directed straight at it. Wilton had seen to opening the windows so fresh air could get in. "I'm sorry this is all we have to offer you," she told him as she began to make up the bed.

"This is fine," Kane assured her as he watched her work. Every time she leaned forward, he caught sight of her behind. It was full and slightly rounded. He knew he should try to sound more appreciative about the room; it was clean and private and the best thing he'd seen in three years.

"Is there anything else I can get you?" she asked Kane, joining him in the center of the room so she could stand up straight without hitting her head.

He gazed at her beneath the naked light bulb. She *was* pretty. Wispy tendrils of dark hair had pulled free from the knot at the back of her head, taking some of the severity out of her hairstyle. Her smooth skin glowed with pale ivory undertones. "I can't think of anything," he said at last.

"Then, if you don't mind, I'll leave you so I can get a bath."

He wished she hadn't said that. Images of her naked wet body reclining in the old porcelain tub downstairs flooded through his mind. His gut tensed. A muscle clenched in his jaw. He didn't need to think of her that way. This was the woman who'd restored his faith in the human race. She was involved with a highly respected man. Besides, she had never offered to be more than his friend. "I appreciate all you've done," he said, forcing a smile he didn't quite feel.

Mel was tempted to tell him he needed to start smiling more instead of wearing that perpetual frown. His handsome face was kindled with a sensual, passionate beauty that made her wonder, once again, why he'd worn that awful beard. His dark eyes held her captive for a moment, making her aware of how alone they were.

"You're very welcome," she said, offering him a tentative smile in return. She felt close to him for reasons she didn't understand. Perhaps it was some displaced maternal instinct that made her want to see to his comforts after what he'd been through. How many nights had she lain in bed and wondered about him, whether he was getting enough to eat or if he was able to go outside for fresh air and exercise. He obviously had. He was in perfect physical condition.

She wished she hadn't had that last thought. In some ways she had been less tense with the beard. Now she was having a heck of a time acting casual when all she really wanted to do was stare. "Well, I'd better go," she said, although she was reluctant to do so.

Kane waited. His gaze clung to hers expectantly. There seemed to be so much more to say. To share. He would have given anything to be able to pull her hair free and run his fingers through it. Even Blair's golden hair—which he suspected came straight out of a bottle—had not tempted him so.

He could not resist touching her face again.

Kane raised his hand to her cheek and cupped it gently. "Do you mind?" he said, when at first she looked surprised and anxious. When she relaxed, he drew his fingers down her face. The texture made him think of honey that had somehow solidified. Her cheekbones were high and delicate, her brows dark and finely arched. She was lovely in a way that made a man think of spring flowers and a rolling green meadow, lovely in a way that made him wonder what she would look like first thing in the morning when she opened her green eyes.

Kane traced her mouth with his thumb, following the bow-shaped upper lip and testing the full bottom one. They were the color of ripened peaches. Finally, because he couldn't resist tasting them, he ducked his head and pressed his own lips to them.

The kiss started out innocently enough but shattered his calm the second their mouths touched. He'd forgotten how good a woman could taste, how sweet. He moved his mouth over hers, at first caressing, then devouring, its softness and sinking his tongue inside. The sensation was like sucking on hard candy all day and finally reaching the juicy center. He could lose himself in the taste and texture of those lips.

The kiss deepened, becoming hot and urgent.

At first Mel was too surprised to do more than let him kiss her. Curiosity, and that ever-present feeling of restlessness, had induced her to part her lips when his tongue pressed against the seam of her mouth. She wasn't sure when the kiss got out of hand, but it did, and before she knew it, he was grinding his lower body against hers. She tried to push him away. It was like trying to move a concrete wall. Fear touched her heart.

Kane snapped his head up when he felt her resist. He took a step back and raked his hands through his hair. He was afraid. Not of being slapped or reprimanded but of losing control.

"I'm sorry," he said, noting how hard and eager his body was. He yearned for that part of her that was slick and wet. He wanted to kiss her until she forgot about her prim upbringing and returned his affections. But he wouldn't. He could no more force himself on a woman than he could walk on water. "You'd better go," he said at last.

Mel didn't miss the warning in his words. Without hesitating, she slipped out the door and stumbled down the stairs on trembling legs. She didn't stop until she'd reached the safety of her own room.

FIVE

Kane sat on the edge of his bed in his underwear and tried to convince himself there was enough air in the attic. Prison had made him claustrophobic, and he hated it because he considered it a weakness. It was bad enough he had this problem dealing with anger. Why did he have to be afraid of tight spaces as well?

He tried to think of something else. He wondered where Mel's room was, wondered if she was asleep or if she was having trouble drifting off too. He hadn't stopped thinking about that kiss. As innocent as it had started out, he knew he would have preferred to keep on kissing her. And that kind of thinking was dangerous. Not only because he wasn't ready to deal with a woman at the moment, but because that woman was already spoken for. He didn't need the complications. What he *did* need was to get his own life together before he involved anyone else.

Those weren't the only reasons he was reluctant to start a relationship, he knew. While his body would have eagerly welcomed a soft, sweet-smelling female, he was not prepared for it emotionally.

Prison had taught him not to feel or care about anything or anybody. If a prisoner was being raped in the basement, it was best just to block it out, rather than to try to do something about it and get a shank in your belly. If the warden demanded a full-scale body search, it was best to pretend it was happening to somebody else. He'd learned long ago, as far back as his dealings with his old man, not to let the next guy know what he was thinking.

It was important to survival.

Kane continued to sit on the bed, even as his mind began to play tricks on him. No, the room was *not* shrinking, and, yes, there was *more* than enough oxygen. He could leave any time he felt like it. He was *not* locked in. He stood and walked to the center of the room where the ceiling was highest.

He took a deep breath.

He remembered again his last conversation with the warden.

"A man fitting your description robbed a Memphis convenience store . . . confessed to a number of crimes, including the one for which you were convicted. His story checked out. He knew things . . ."

Kane hadn't responded right away. He'd merely stroked his beard and fixed the man with a glacial stare. In a world where everything had a price and must be bargained for, his long poker face had served him well and earned him grudging respect from some of the most hardened criminals. "So what are you saying?" he'd asked after a brittle silence.

"I'm telling you, Mr. Stoddard, that as soon as we process your paperwork, you're a free man."

Kane's eyes registered disbelief. Freedom. It was the sweetest word he knew, and he had dreamed of this moment for three long years. Thirty-six endless months. It was too good to be true, a damn miracle.

But miracles didn't happen to people like him.

Suddenly, his mind raced with strange and disquieting thoughts. Was he being set up? Did somebody want something from him? He didn't have a clue in hell what it could be. Maybe he was being paranoid, he told himself. If the warden wanted information, he would simply try to strike a deal. But then, the warden knew from experience Kane Stoddard didn't strike deals or snitch, even when it served his purpose, even when it meant sure punishment not to.

"Are you sure?" he said at last.

"I'm sure, Mr. Stoddard. I wouldn't have called you in here otherwise."

Kane's thoughts were already headed in another direction. The system had made a mistake. "So that's it?" he asked. "What about the fact that I've been screwed out of three years of my life? Am I just supposed to pretend it didn't happen?"

The warden tugged at his shirt collar as though he suddenly found it too tight. Beads of sweat dotted his forehead and upper lip.

"It's up to you if you want to obtain legal counsel, Mr. Stoddard," he said.

Kane gave a snort of disgust. "With two hundred and fifty bucks in my pocket?" he asked, knowing that's all the money they were required to give him when he left. That, and the clothes he'd had on his back.

The other man took off his glasses and began to clean the lens with a tissue. He held the glasses to the light and inspected them. "I did not prosecute you, Mr. Stoddard, but one only has to look at your record to understand why a jury had no problem finding you guilty. You've been in and out of trouble all your life."

Kane would have enjoyed shoving those glasses down the man's throat. "And I paid for every offense," he said, his chest growing tight with anger. That same anger had been the focus of most of his visits with the prison psychologist. "This time I paid for something I didn't do."

The warden put on his glasses once more. "I'll admit our legal system isn't perfect. You're not the first man to be wrongly accused and convicted of a crime. But I had nothing to do with that. My job was to offer you the best conditions in which to serve your time. Which is exactly what I did, what with the counseling and educational benefits you received." He paused. "But we can't change your attitude, Mr. Stoddard, and if you don't lose that attitude, I'll give you six months before you're back."

His rage hit with lightning-quick speed. Kane had clenched his fists at his sides, fighting the urge to punch the man square in the jaw. This man, in his polyester gabardine suit, had no idea what it was like to live in that prison. "I'll see you in hell first," he'd replied.

Now, as Kane stood in the tiny attic, the warden's warning echoed in his head.

"I'll give you six months."

The thought of going back to prison turned his blood cold. He would prefer death to that. Which was another reason he'd chosen Hardeeville, Mississippi, for his new home instead of returning to Memphis and his old friends who would probably land him in jail before long.

No, he would never go back. And one day, hopefully soon, he would be able to rise in the morning without thinking about it and lie down at night without dreaming about it.

Kane raked his hands through his hair and tried to think of something else. Anything. He spied the stack of photo albums near the wall and couldn't resist picking one up. He carried the album to his bed and opened it. The photos were old and faded, some having yellowed with age. Kane recognized no one. He turned the page. A young woman, no more than a girl actually, stared back at him from a tattered newspaper clipping that announced her engagement to Wilton Abercrombie. Mel's mother, he thought, studying the picture for some signs of resemblance. He decided she looked more like Blair. At the bottom of the page he found that same young woman standing beside a man he recognized as a younger, thinner version of Wilton. He noticed the age difference immediately. Wilton had taken himself a child bride.

The next page showed her being wheeled out of a hospital with a baby in her arms. He grinned at the pictures that followed of Melanie Abercrombie, a plump baby wearing a spit curl in the center of her head. He followed her progress on the next few pages; her first Christmas, her first birthday. There were pictures of Mel in the bathtub, Mel taking her first steps, and Mel using the potty.

He chuckled at the sight. Melanie Abercrombie would have a fit if she knew he was looking at her baby pictures.

A newborn Blair appeared about midway through the photo album, and from then on the pictures consisted of two girls and a young mother who looked tired and frazzled much of the time. Kane finished looking through that photo album and went for another. This time the girls had entered elementary school. He followed their progress, then realized when he was almost to the end of the album that he hadn't seen their mother's picture for some time. There were pictures of Wilton and various other faces, but the young woman who'd given birth to the little girls was nowhere to be found. Kane closed the album. He didn't want to have to think about the hurt Mel had suffered over her mother's abandonment. Not tonight, when there were so many other things he had to worry about, such as finding a job and a place to live. Not when he had so many bad memories of his own.

Finally, the attic got to be too much for him. Kane knew he had to get the hell out of there or go crazy. He shrugged on his clothes and dug through his duffel bag for his old sneakers. A moment later he tiptoed down the stairs and slipped out the back door of the house.

He stood on the back steps, sucking in the night air like one who'd been deprived of oxygen for a long time. The sky was littered with stars. It was exhilarating knowing he could step outside any time he wished. Using the light of the full moon, he walked around to the front of the house and started for the road. He was tense all over.

He began to run. The air was cool, fanning his face. His muscles were stiff. He'd missed his daily run since he'd gotten out. His counselor had taught him several years ago to use his anger and frustration in ways that would help him instead of hurt. He had taken up jogging and weight lifting as a result. Not only had it relieved tension, he was healthier today because of it.

There was a big difference between jogging on the prison track and running along the open road with the wind in his face. That made him more determined never to return to prison. He would find a job and a place to live, and he'd keep his nose clean because freedom was more important than anything else.

Kane ran for another fifteen minutes, then turned back for the Abercrombie house. His breathing was measured, his pace steady. A sense of euphoria swept over him, and he felt he could run forever. He didn't see the hole in the road. All he knew was that when his foot came down, it didn't make contact with the asphalt. Instead, it landed in a pothole. He tried to break his fall, but he twisted his ankle so badly, it popped.

The pain was excruciating, and at first he thought he might throw up. He muttered a mouthful of obscenities and wondered how he was going to make it back to the house on one foot.

❖━━━❖

Mel gazed down at the sleeping man and wondered what had possessed him to leave the attic and sleep outside on her father's hammock in the backyard, when it was obvious the mosquitoes had had a field day with him. His face bore the evidence of several welts. Looking at that handsome face made her think of the kiss they'd shared, the same kiss that had caused her to lie awake half the night and stare at the dark ceiling. She let her gaze take in the rest of him, the broad shoulders, the strong, muscular body, his powerful thighs. She gasped at the sight of his swollen ankle.

"Kane?" She shook him gently.

Kane's eyes flew open, and he bolted upright with a start, looking for all the world as though he were ready for a fight. He winced as pain shot through his ankle. "What do you want?" he demanded, his mood sour from spending the night in a hammock and offering up his flesh to every mosquito within a five-mile radius.

"What are you doing out here?" she asked. "And what on earth happened to your ankle?"

Kane glanced in the direction of his feet and saw the ankle had grown worse during the night. It had hurt like the devil all night long, but he hadn't wanted to wake anyone in the house. He figured the hammock would be more comfortable than the attic. Still, he hadn't fallen asleep until shortly before dawn.

"I sprained it," he said, noting how fresh Mel looked in a straight denim skirt and white blouse. He explained how he couldn't sleep and had decided to go jogging.

"In the dark?"

"Yeah." He'd already told himself he was dumber than cow dung for doing it.

"Can you put any weight on it?"

He shot her a pained look. "I suppose I could. But somebody would have to put a gun to my head to get me to do it."

She chuckled. "Just stay put for a minute. I'll get Daddy out here."

Kane opened his mouth to protest, but she was gone before he could get the words out. She returned a moment later with Wilton, who was wearing a checkered bathrobe. Kane was forced to repeat the story of how he'd stepped in a hole in the road while jogging.

"He probably needs to see a doctor," Wilton said, helping Kane up and positioning himself under one arm while Mel did the same on the other side. Together, they managed to get him inside.

"It's just a sprain," Kane assured them as he took a seat at the kitchen table.

Mel was already pulling an ice tray from the freezer. "I'll put ice on it," she said. "If that doesn't help, I'll call Dr. Hadley."

When Blair stumbled into the kitchen half-asleep twenty minutes later, Kane was sitting in one chair, his foot propped on another with an ice pack on it. "What happened to you?" she asked in a voice that suggested whatever it was, it had to be illegal.

"Kane sprained his ankle," Mel told her. "He went jogging and stepped in a hole in the road."

Blair went straight for the coffeepot and poured herself a cup. "So how's he supposed to find a job with a bad ankle?"

Mel saw the hard look Kane shot Blair and knew he was on the verge of erupting. Why did Blair have to push him? "I'm sure Kane didn't sprain it on purpose," she said. "Besides, with the proper care, it'll heal in no time."

"It's beginning to feel better already," Kane said, his mouth pressed into a grim line. He tried to stand, then winced, wondering how he was going to operate the clutch on his bike. Still, anything was better than dealing with this snotty creature before him. "If ya'll don't mind, I think I'll hit the road," he said, his voice edged with anger.

Wilton walked into the room at the perfect time and placed a restraining hand on his shoulder. "You're not going anywhere till that ankle is better. Mel can fix up the sofa so you can rest there." His tone of voice suggested there was no room for debate.

Kane hesitated. Although he was in a hurry to escape the mouthy blonde and get on with his life, he wasn't ready to say good-bye to Mel just yet.

"And I'll drop by at lunch and fix you a sandwich," she said, when Kane seemed to be weakening. She smiled brightly. "Please stay. At least until you heal."

His gaze locked with hers. When she smiled like that, he felt it right in the pit of his stomach. He wondered how two sisters had turned out so differently. "Thanks," he said, promising himself he would be more tolerant of Blair. "I'd like that."

"What about *me*?" Blair said, drawing a look from all three of them. "You're not going to leave me here *alone* with *him*."

"I'm afraid we have no choice," Wilton said, then winked at Kane. "Call me at the store if she gives you any trouble."

Petals-n-Things was located across the street from the courthouse and tucked between Nel's Piece Goods and Mike's Bikes. Mel pushed open the old-fashioned beveled glass door and sent the tiny bell above into a wild frenzy.

"Be with you in a sec," Mel's assistant called out from the back room.

"It's just me," Mel replied.

Eunice Jenkins appeared in the doorway wearing knit leggings, an oversized blouse, and a crocheted vest. Her flame-red hair, which was teased out to there, looked as though it might crack under the weight of so much hair spray. She held a basket of pink and white African violets. Unlike her clothing, they had been tastefully arranged.

"Guess what?" she said, her voice conspiratorial. "Ed Higginbothom called me at home, got me out of the bed, to order flowers for his wife. You ask me, I think he's feeling guilty about those long lunches with his secretary. Only they don't call themselves secretaries these days. They're administrative assistants."

Mel set her purse on the counter. "What makes you think Mr. Higginbothom and his secretary weren't discussing business during these lunches?"

Eunice gave a snort of disgust. "Well, honey, I've been married three times. I reckon I know a little bit about men, and what I do know is most of them are scum and will cheat if given half a chance."

"Ed and Martha Higginbothom have been happily married for twenty years. I don't know a couple more suited."

"How do you *know* they're happy? How do you

know they aren't staying together because they're mortgaged to their belly buttons? Or maybe they're staying together for the sake of the kids."

Mel didn't quite know how to respond. Eunice made no secret that she hated men, and she thought Mel's dreams of marriage and children naive.

She decided she would not tell Eunice about Kane after all.

"So how's business this morning?" she asked instead.

"You know it's too early to tell. But I imagine it's going to be slow after what we went through with Easter and the prom. Which brings me to the next question. *Why* are you here? I thought you were going to spend the next couple of weeks remodeling your dad's store while I took care of this place. What's changed? It's only been two days."

"Would you believe I missed you?" Mel said, still feeling the need to talk to someone about Kane. But who?

Eunice picked up Mel's purse and handed it to her. "No. What I *do* believe is that you sometimes get neurotic about this place. Stop worrying. Tell me one thing *you* do that *I* can't do."

Mel knew there was nothing. Eunice had been with her from the first day she opened the flower shop eight years earlier. They might be vastly different in personality, but they both knew the flower business.

"Okay, I'll leave," she said, wishing Eunice were not so hard so communicate with at times. "But you promise to call me if you need me?"

"You know I will. Now go!"

When Mel arrived back at the house for lunch, she found Kane sitting at the kitchen table with the newspaper opened to the classified section. He looked pleased with himself. "I've already set up two job interviews for tomorrow."

"So soon? Do you think you'll be walking by then?"

"I'll be okay. I've waited three years to get my life together. I'm not going to let a bum ankle stop me."

Mel was glad to see he had a positive attitude. She pulled out the ingredients for sandwiches. "Where's Blair?"

He shrugged and went back to his newspaper. "In her room, I reckon. I think she's avoiding me." He looked up at Mel and grinned. "What do you think?"

Mel was tempted to tell him that when he smiled that way he was the handsomest man alive. "Blair's angry with me right now," she said instead. "Don't let her take it out on you."

"Why's she mad at you?"

She reached for the bread. "I haven't spent much

time with her since she's been back. What with remodeling the store and all," she added. "I know she's having it rough right now, but she picked the worst possible time to come home. Still, I'm going to have to *make* time for her. I can tell she's depressed."

"I'd be depressed, too, if I slept all day," Kane told her, folding the newspaper and setting it aside. "Doesn't she have friends she can visit?"

Mel chuckled. "You mean the *local yokels*, as Blair refers to them? No, she doesn't have friends in Hardeeville." She handed him a plate bearing two bologna and cheese sandwiches and a handful of potato chips. He thanked her. "What's worse, she doesn't have a car and hasn't bothered to renew her driver's license since she moved to New York." She sighed as she poured them each a glass of iced tea. "I wish there was something I could do to help her. I hate seeing her so miserable."

"Maybe it's time you stopped acting like her mother."

"I'm not acting like her mother," she replied. "How can you possibly make that sort of judgment? You barely know us."

Kane put his sandwich down and took a swig of tea. "You're right about that," he said. "But I don't have to be a rocket scientist to see that you're acting like a parent toward her."

"What are you, an undercover psychologist?"

He shook his head. "I spent a little time with the

prison psychologist. Once or twice a week for three years as a matter of fact."

His confession surprised her. Her tone softened. "Did it help?"

He shrugged. "I reckon. I used to be angry a lot. Put my hand through a few walls in my time. Not to mention my share of windows." He saw her wince. "Now it's not so bad."

"Is that why you were out jogging in the middle of the night? To relieve your anger?"

His gaze locked with hers. His hooded expression prolonged the moment. "No, anger had nothing to do with it. My restlessness was all because of you."

Mel gazed back at him for a full minute, not knowing how to respond. What *could* she say? That *she, too*, had lain awake thinking of *him*?

She decided the best way to handle it was to change the subject. "Would you like another sandwich?"

The mood was broken. Kane knew she had done it intentionally. "Naw. And I don't want you to think you have to wait on me hand and foot while I'm here. I may not win any races over the next couple of days, but I can still get around."

"The less you walk on it, the faster it's going to heal."

"Which is why I put off those interviews until tomorrow," he said. He glanced at the clock on the wall. "Don't you have to get back to the store?"

he asked, not wanting her to feel obligated to sit with him when she obviously had a lot to do. He suspected she had more obligations than she could handle. When she nodded, he went on. "How's the remodeling going?"

She stifled the urge to moan aloud. She had given up on the carpenter she'd hired over the phone and was in the process of interviewing others. The only problem was, they were much more expensive and couldn't start for weeks. "I'm sure we'll manage," she said, giving nothing away.

Mel carried their plates to the sink and picked up the sack lunch she'd prepared for her father. "I should be heading back," she told him. "See you later." She could feel his black eyes boring into her as she walked away.

SIX

Mel checked each of the simple multiplication problems and saw they were correct. "Very good, Amy," she told the freckled-faced eight-year-old. "Your math teacher will be pleased."

Amy beamed. "I won the timed quiz today," she said. "Miss Robbins gave us twenty-five multiplication problems, and I finished first. I got a coupon for two free chili dogs at the Salty Dog Sandwich Shop, and Principal Barnes announced it over the loudspeaker at the end of the day."

"Congratulations!" Mel couldn't have been more proud. When she'd met Amy six months ago, the girl had been depressed and withdrawn as a result of her mother's death the previous year. Her grades had suffered as well. Mel decided then and there that she and Amy's father—whom she had already dated a couple of times—would proceed with caution in their relationship. Amy needed a friend right now more than anything.

"Okay, Miss Whiz Kid," Mel said. "What other homework do you have?"

"I have to study for my spelling test."

"I'll call out the words while I prepare the casserole." Mel glanced at her wristwatch as she went to the refrigerator. Harper had asked her to pick up Amy from her after-school baby-sitter so he could attend a last-minute meeting at work. It wasn't the first time Mel had done so, and she certainly didn't mind doing the small favor, but she was distracted today for reasons she couldn't explain.

Kane had left that morning, still hobbling about on his bad foot, and she had worried about him for the rest of the day. What if he didn't find a job right away? What if his ankle got worse?

Mel called out Amy's spelling words while she prepared a broccoli-and-chicken casserole and put it into the oven to bake. She was in the process of putting a load of towels into the washer when Harper walked through the front door. He was as blond as his daughter, though his hair was already thinning. While he wasn't a handsome man, he looked distinguished in his business suit. Without the jacket, though, one could see he was already growing soft in the middle.

The look on his face gave Mel pause.

"Harper, what's wrong?"

"Tell me it isn't true," he said without preamble.

Mel tried to figure out what he was talking about. She couldn't. "Tell you *what* isn't true, Harper?"

"Tell me you don't *really* have an ex-con living in your house."

Mel pulled out of Harper's driveway a few minutes later, after assuring him Kane was gone, and headed for town and a section of low-income housing where someone had reported a stray dog. As she paused at the only red light in town, located between the courthouse and her flower shop, she resisted the urge to drop in and check on Eunice before she went home for the day. Her assistant would only accuse her of being neurotic again; then she'd spend the next hour telling her how sorry men were. As much as she loved Eunice and appreciated her hard work, Mel wearied of her negative comments regarding the opposite sex.

She concentrated instead on the lovely flower gardens adorning the courthouse lawn. A longtime member of the Women's Garden Club, Mel assisted with the selection and planting of the flowers. This year they had accented the coleus and impatiens with white candytuft, and the look was stunning.

The light changed but not before Mel noticed the massive motorcycle parked in front of the courthouse and a lone man sitting on a bench nearby. A warm glow flowed through her at the sight of him. She quickly pulled in beside the bike. Kane didn't look up as she approached; he seemed deep in thought.

"Hello, stranger," she called out. "What are you doing out here?"

He glanced up at the sound of her voice, then shifted uneasily on the bench. Although he was glad to see her, she had definitely caught him at a bad time. "Resting my ankle," he said.

"How is it?"

Although the swelling was down, it was still tender. "Fine."

Mel tried to read the look on his face but couldn't. She took a seat beside him. "So, how was your day?"

"Nobody's hiring."

"Really?" She was surprised to hear it. Only this morning he had told her about several places, most of them near town, that sounded promising. Even the Goulds from the print shop had an ad in the paper. The job would have been perfect for him.

"Don't look so shocked," Kane said, reading the expression on her face. "You know as well as I do why they aren't hiring."

Mel clasped her hands tightly in her lap. His black eyes were hooded, and she wondered what emotion he was trying to hide. Pain? Discouragement? She also wondered where he'd learned to disguise his feelings so well. "You were cleared of any wrong-doing, Kane," she said, not bothering to pretend she didn't know *why* folks weren't hiring. "Did you tell them that?"

"Of course I told them that. You know what? It doesn't matter. The fact that I spent three years behind bars, surrounded by rapists and murderers, is enough to scare people." His jaw was hard, his voice contemptuous.

"It didn't scare Daddy or me."

His look softened, and he almost smiled. "You two aren't like most people."

"So, did you find a place to live?" she asked, and watched his face darken once more.

"I went to the boardinghouse you told me about. No vacancy. I don't know if that's for real or if it's just a line of crap. I also called a couple of apartments listed in the paper. They want a month's rent up front, plus deposits for utilities."

"So what are you going to do?" she said, feeling just as frustrated.

"There's a temporary employment agency advertising for construction workers. I've got an appointment with them first thing in the morning. I'm not that thrilled about it, but it's a job until something better comes along."

"Do you know how to do that sort of work?"

"I should. I've been doing it since before I got out of high school."

"What about carpentry work?" she said hopefully. "There's a whole aisle in our store that needs new shelving."

He was thoughtful for a moment. "Wouldn't it be cheaper to put up prefabricated shelves?"

"It wouldn't match the rest of the store, and it would take away from the rustic quality."

"I don't have any tools."

"We've got all the tools," she said. "We've even got a fancy saw. It's just Dad and I aren't very good at doing that kind of work." She paused, waiting for him to say something. "I'll pay you, of course," she added, when he remained quiet. "And you can stay with us. No sense paying for a place until you find a real job."

"How about the rest of your family? What are they going to think about such an arrangement?"

"Oh, Daddy will be thrilled, naturally. As for Blair . . . let me deal with her. I'll even convince her to let me move into her room so you can have mine."

"Which I'm sure she'll be only too happy to do once you tell her it's on account of me," he said sourly.

"Kane, I'm really desperate. My father and I have been tearing down the old shelves for two days. We're at a standstill now because we don't have a carpenter to rebuild them."

"I'll do it," he said. "But I don't want your money. Giving me a place to stay is enough." When she started to protest, he went on. "Besides, it's the least I can do after what you did for me."

He stood as though bringing the discussion to a close. "And one other thing. I may have to take an hour off here and there if I have to go on an interview."

"That's fair."

He held out his hand as though to seal their agreement, and she felt a ripple of excitement when she put her hand in his. It was both disturbing and comforting.

"Ready to go?" he asked, feeling better about his situation already.

"First I have to stop off and pick up a dog."

"Another stray?"

"A mean one."

He surprised her by grinning. "That sounds like fun. I'll leave my bike here and ride with you."

They started for the car with Kane taking it slow because of his ankle. Mel felt more optimistic than she had in days. She finally had someone who could do the work in the store, and it wasn't going to cost her a fortune. Not only that, she was going to be able to help him in the process. That was important to her.

There was only one drawback. She was going to have to tell Harper that Kane had moved back into the house.

———◆———◆———

The Doberman pinscher bared his teeth and snarled menacingly as Mel approached. "Nice dog," she said in a soothing voice. "It's okay, boy."

"I wouldn't get any closer," Kane warned, standing several feet behind her. "He looks about as friendly as a rattlesnake."

"Oh, he's not really so bad, are you, boy?" Mel asked the dog. She came to a halt several feet from the stoop where the animal crouched ready to attack. They stared at each other for a long moment as though sizing each other up. Mel saw that he was pitifully skinny. Nevertheless, it didn't prevent him from looking vicious.

Mel folded her hands in front of her and waited for the dog to calm down. "It's okay, boy," she said. "I'm not going to hurt you. I know you've had it rough these past few days, what with your master dying and all." The dog cocked his head to the side as though trying to understand what she was saying.

Kane watched the exchange anxiously. He'd been bitten by a large dog as a kid, and he didn't want to relive the event in his adulthood. "Did his owner really die?" he asked quietly, not wanting to excite the animal.

She nodded. "Three days ago. His name was Elmer Dinsberry. Meanest man who ever walked the face of this earth. And this poor fellow has been sitting right here waiting for him to return ever since, though I can't imagine why."

The dog continued to watch her carefully. Mel reached into her pocket for a dog biscuit. She carried a box in her car for just this reason. Placing it on the edge of the stoop, she took a step back and waited. The dog sniffed it cautiously, backed away for a moment, then pounced on it, taking it between his teeth and literally gobbling it down as though afraid someone would take it from him.

"That's a good boy," Mel said, reaching into her pocket for another. "I don't think you're so mean. I think you're pretty nice to sit here day after day waiting for your master to come back when he wasn't very nice to you to begin with."

"What do you mean?" Kane asked, never taking his eyes off the huge animal, planning what he'd do if he turned on Mel.

"Old Elmer mistreated him," she said. "The lady across the street told me all sorts of horrible things. It's no wonder the poor dog doesn't trust anyone." She handed him another biscuit. This time he took it right from her hand.

"Be careful," Kane said. Even though the dog was no longer snarling, the hair was still raised along his backbone.

Mel waited until the animal finished eating, then allowed him to sniff her fingers. Time passed. He wasn't as tense now. She patted his head, then stroked him, all the while talking to him in a tone that inspired confidence. Finally, he wagged his nubby tail.

Kane merely watched.

"You want to go for a ride, fellow?" she asked.

All at once the Doberman jumped from the stoop and made for the car as though he understood perfectly. He barked, wagged his tail again, and waited.

"Well, I'll be damned," Kane said.

It wasn't until after they'd returned home that Mel and Kane realized they faced the dilemma of what they were going to do with the dog.

"You're not going to put him in the pen with the other dogs, are you?" Kane said, thinking of the puppy.

Mel thought for a moment, then disappeared into the garage. She emerged a few minutes later carrying a coiled rope, a metal stake, and a hammer. "I'm going to have to tie him up, I'm afraid. Would you put this in the ground beside that tall oak? That way he'll have plenty of shade."

As Kane pounded the stake in the ground, Mel fastened one end of the rope to the dog's collar while he growled under his breath. "It's okay, boy," she said. "It's a long rope, and you'll be able to walk around."

Kane tied the other end of the rope to the stake while Mel hurried into the house for food and water.

She set it before the dog and watched as the animal wolfed it down. "Poor thing," she said, keeping a respectful distance as he ate. "No telling when he last ate."

"It won't be easy finding him a home, will it?" Kane asked, coming up beside her.

"You're right about that. Nobody wants a grown Doberman pinscher with an attitude when they can have a cute little puppy." She studied the animal. "What I don't understand is why he hung around when he was being mistreated. Why didn't he run away?"

Kane shrugged. "Maybe he thought he deserved it."

"Nobody deserves to be mistreated."

Kane pondered it. He could remember being knocked around by his old man so much as a kid that he thought he deserved it. He must be some rotten kid to stay in so much trouble. Then he realized his brothers and sisters were getting knocked around too. It came as no surprise when all the kids scattered as soon as they reached legal age. "He eats like a horse," he said, changing the subject so he didn't have to think about the past and the fact he hadn't seen some of his siblings in almost fifteen years. "Nobody's going to want him. Pretty hopeless, if you ask me."

"There's always hope," she said with conviction.

He shot her a curious look. "Even for a sorry excuse like myself, Miss Abercrombie?"

"*Especially* for you."

Kane studied her, not quite knowing what to say. He'd never met anyone like her. Why was she so determined to save him? He found himself stepping closer in an attempt to get a better look at those green eyes. They sparkled like gems. She had a healthy glow about her.

"You're staring," she stated flatly.

"Do you mind?"

"It makes me uncomfortable."

"Why, because of that Harper fellow?"

She knew Harper had nothing to do with it. "Because I'm not used to it."

"You should be. You *would* be if you'd dump those old-lady clothes you wear and let your hair down. You don't need them any more than you needed those ugly glasses."

She was offended by his criticism of her clothes. "I'm sorry if you don't like the way I dress. I'm very comfortable this way."

"Know what I think?" He crossed his arms and regarded her. "I think you're afraid to look good. Who knows, folks might start comparing you to your sister."

"That's ridiculous, there is no comparison. Blair's beautiful."

"So are you."

Mel realized she was holding her breath. "Three years is a long time to be out of circulation. I reckon a man will say anything to turn a woman's head. But I don't appreciate being made fun of, Mr. Stoddard. Now, if you'll excuse me, I need to start dinner."

Kane reached out and closed one hand around her wrist and brought her to an immediate halt. "Let's get one thing straight," he said, his words clipped and concise. "I don't do or say anything that I don't want to, and if I was looking to get laid, I assure you I could find someone willing."

She didn't doubt it. "What do you want from me, Kane?" she asked, at a loss to figure him out.

"Are you in love with that Harper fellow you've been seeing?"

"What business is that of yours?"

"I'm making it my business."

She tried to pull free but couldn't. "He's a good man, and we have similar interests."

"And you can't think of a damn thing you'd have in common with an ex-con."

"I didn't say that."

He pulled her closer. "Do your toes curl when he makes love to you?"

Her first instinct was to slap him. Mel raised her hand, but he caught it. "You are clearly out of line," she said.

"You saved me," he said. "I feel it's my duty to return the favor." Still holding both hands, he pulled her against him. Her mouth flew open in protest, and he used it to his advantage, capturing her lips and sinking his tongue inside. He kissed her hungrily, greedily, crushing her against him so there was no doubt how quickly he'd become aroused. Mel squirmed in his arms, but there was no escape. Finally, he released her.

Shame surged through her as she stared back at the dark face with glittering black eyes. She had never, *ever* been kissed like that before. "Who do you think you are?" she demanded, trembling from head to foot. "What gives you the right?"

He offered her a cocky smile, but inside his guts were shaking from wanting her. "Nobody gave me the right to kiss you. I took it 'cause I figured you needed kissing." He paused and fixed her with a lethal stare. "And if you don't leave right now, I'm going to kiss you again."

"You expect me to do *what*!" Blair demanded in such a way one would have thought she had been asked to dance naked in the vegetable garden.

Mel fidgeted with the buttons on her blouse. She'd expected Blair to be upset, but she hadn't expected it to turn into a shouting match. "I told you, I need for you to let me move into your room for a few days while Kane stays in my room."

"Why is he staying here, Mel? Have you completely lost your mind?"

"He's offered to help remodel the store. The least

we can do is offer him a place to stay. Besides, he hasn't had any luck finding a place in town."

"Oh, you make me sick with this Goody Two-shoes act you put on," Blair said with an air of disgust. "Good old Mel, always doing for other people. Why is it you never have time for your own family?"

"What do you want from me, Blair?" she said wearily.

"I want you to listen to me, that's what! I want you to forget about Harper and the dogs and your ex-con and just listen to *me* for a change. *I* need your help now."

"Help with what, for heaven's sake?"

"Help me make a few decisions, that's what." Blair was shouting now. Tears filled her eyes, and she swiped at them angrily. "I'm scared, Mel. Terrified. My career is going to hell, and I need advice. I want to know whether I should give it up completely or dump my agent and hire someone who's more excited about me."

"I can't advise you on your career."

Blair took a deep, shuddering breath. "And I want to know what to do with this child I'm carrying."

Mel's head snapped up. "What!"

Her younger sister burst into tears and flung herself across the bed. "That's why I came home," she cried, her words muffled by a pillow. "I'm pregnant."

"Pregnant!" Mel sank onto the bed beside her,

then sat in stunned silence. "I didn't even know you were in love with anybody," she said after a moment.

Blair groaned aloud, rolled onto her back, and regarded her sister. "Grow up," she said in between sobs.

Mel tried for a more sophisticated approach. "Weren't you using protection?"

"Of course I was using protection. I guess that means it wasn't foolproof."

"How far along are you?"

Blair pushed herself into a sitting position and wiped her eyes. "Six weeks. I made an appointment to get an abortion while I was in New York, but I couldn't go through with it. Now I wish I had. I've never been so sick in my life."

The last thing Mel wanted to discuss with her sister was an abortion. "What about the baby's father?" she asked instead. "What does he say about all this?"

Blair gave a snort of disgust. "He's the one who gave me the money for the abortion. Said if I didn't go through with it, I was on my own. Besides, he's already got children." She paused. "And a wife as well."

At first Mel was not certain she'd heard right. It was incomprehensible. Painful fingers squeezed her heart. She steeled herself for the truth. "How can that be, Blair?" she asked, forcing herself to remain calm.

Fresh tears filled Blair's eyes. "Oh, Mel, you don't really know anything about life at all."

She was tired of hearing how naive she was. "Since when has sleeping with another woman's husband constituted a great knowledge of life?" she asked.

Blair pulled away. "I don't need you to preach to me. I know I made a mistake, but I'll be the one to pay."

Mel was quiet for a moment. Blair was right. The damage was done, and this was a time for action, not recrimination. "I hate for you to view an innocent baby as punishment. Who knows, a baby could change your life for the better."

Blair rolled her eyes heavenward. "Yes, well, try modeling a bikini with a kid in your belly."

"You'll have to take some time off. It wouldn't be the end of the world." Mel knew it wasn't as simple as that, but they would have to take it one day at a time. They would have months to work out the details.

"I need time to think about this some more," Blair said. "Don't say anything to Daddy about it right now."

"Of course not."

"In the meantime, don't expect me to be as thrilled about it as you are."

Mel sighed. Knowing her sister as she did, she imagined she would make herself and everybody else as miserable as possible over the next few days. "So is it okay if I move in with you for a while?" she asked, knowing she would have to deal with her sister's unhappiness at close range.

"You might as well," Blair grumbled. "The rest of my life has gone to hell."

Mel led Kane into her bedroom as soon as dinner was over with. Although she hadn't said anything about the kiss, she was cool toward him and hoped the message was clear that she would not tolerate a replay of what had happened earlier. Her tone was all business. "I've put fresh sheets on the bed and made room for your clothes in my closet."

Kane studied the room in silence. Its mint-green decor was soothing, the four-poster bed cozy and inviting. "I feel guilty as hell taking your bed," he said.

"That's okay. Blair has twin beds in her room, and she's agreed to let me move in with her." She didn't need to add how unhappy Blair was at the prospect; it was obvious the girl was pouting because she had refused to come to dinner. Mel was going to have a little talk with her about her dieting. Now that Blair was pregnant, she couldn't go on with her erratic eating habits.

"I've also emptied this top drawer," she said, pointing to a bureau. "You may use it while you're here."

"Mel?"

"If there's nothing else—"

Kane closed the distance between them. "I'm sorry about the kiss," he said, and watched her cheeks flame in response. She glanced away. "I mean, I'm not sorry because I didn't enjoy it. I enjoyed it very much. I'm just sorry if I insulted you. I don't know what came over me."

An uncomfortable silence ensued. "I feel very protective of you for some reason," he said. "I suppose it's because of what you did for me, all the letters you wrote. That place was so bad, you can't imagine. Your letters sort of restored my faith in people and gave me the strength to make it through another day. I guess I want to know that you're happy with your life."

Mel was touched to the core by his apology. "I accept your apology, Kane, and I thank you for it. As for my happiness, I'm very content with my life. I know it probably seems dull, my living with my father all these years, but it's what I wanted. I'm not the free spirit Blair is. I've never had the desire to travel to distant places because I'm happy to make the most of where I am."

"And this Harper fellow shares your opinion?"

"Yes."

"What does he think of me being here?"

"He doesn't know you're back."

"Are you sure I should hang around?"

"Why don't you let me handle Harper." She walked toward the door.

Kane watched her. She was tall and straight and moved so gracefully. He enjoyed watching her walk. But not half as much as he'd enjoyed kissing her.

"Good night, Mel," he said softly.

She smiled and slipped out the door.

SEVEN

Kane started work the next day, measuring carefully so he could determine exactly how much lumber he would need for the job. The old shelves had been built of solid oak, obviously at a time when lumber costs weren't soaring. He decided on a cheaper grade of wood, knowing once it was painted, folks wouldn't know the difference. Besides, the Abercrombies weren't wealthy people. He figured they would appreciate the savings. From the looks of it they had obviously put off replacing the old shelves as long as they could.

"What do you think?" Mel asked, having remained silent while Kane had measured the job.

"This should about do it." He handed her the list of what they'd need.

"We can go to the lumber store in Daddy's truck," she said. "Let me get his keys."

Once they were outside, Mel tossed Kane the keys. "You haven't forgotten how to drive, have you?"

He caught the keys in one hand and grinned. "Some things you never forget." Still, he was touched that she trusted him to drive her father's truck.

They were on their way in a matter of minutes with Mel giving him brief directions to the lumber store. "So how'd you sleep last night?" she asked. They hadn't had a chance to talk much.

"Your bed is very comfortable," he said, avoiding the question. He hadn't slept very well at all. Too much on his mind, he supposed. And he'd had another dream. Every time he closed his eyes, he dreamed of that godforsaken place, then woke up in a cold sweat. "And you?" he asked, noting how fresh she looked in a white cotton pullover and slacks that were creased straight as a yardstick.

"I slept okay," she said. Mel wasn't about to tell him how Blair had kept her up half the night talking about how much she hated her life. She'd insisted Blair eat a sandwich before going to bed, then listened as her sister became immediately sick in the bathroom. She decided then and there to get Blair to a doctor first chance she got.

"You look as if you have a lot on your mind today," Kane said, noting how thoughtful she was.

Mel glanced at him. It would have been so much easier to be friends with him if he hadn't kissed her those couple of times. As it was, she found herself reacting to the undeniable magnetism building between them. It frightened her because no matter how eager he seemed to get a job and settle down, she sensed a restlessness about him. Would he be content to live out his days in Hardeeville, or would he, like Blair, yearn for bigger things? "I suppose I do have a lot on my mind," she said at last.

"You want to talk about it?"

She longed to confide in him, not only about Blair but other things as well. She wished she could tell him about the unopened letters in her lingerie drawer and make him understand *why* she was hiding them. She wished she could tell him how excited she was because there was a baby on the way, a niece or nephew, but she couldn't tell him that either. The intermittent guilt and excitement was making her a nervous wreck. "I can't talk about it right now," she said. She looked at him. "But believe me, when I can, you'll be the first to know."

That thought warmed him.

The lumber store was already bustling with customers when they arrived. Mel went straight to the service counter where Homer Bledsoe was telling someone about the new fiberglass screen they had in stock. He saw Mel and smiled. Homer's wife had died several years back, and he made no secret he was looking for a replacement. Only problem was, he lived with his mother, a crotchety woman of seventy who suffered spells where she refused to wear clothes. It was not unusual for the neighbors to see her checking the mail in her underwear.

"What brings you in today, Mel?" he said.

She returned the smile. "I guess you heard we're remodeling." He nodded, and she handed him the list. "I need to order lumber for the shelves." She paused. "You probably need to talk to the man who's going to build them." She introduced him to Kane and watched Homer's smile fade abruptly. Mel couldn't help but wonder how he'd found out about Kane so quickly.

Homer studied the list, glancing up every now and then at Kane. He turned to Mel. "You know Bernice Wyatt's son is looking for contracting work. He's a good man with a family to support. He'd have given you a fair price."

"That's nice of you to tell me, Homer, but Mr. Stoddard has agreed to do the work. Will it take long to fill the order?"

Homer glanced at his wristwatch as though he suddenly realized he had to be somewhere else. "I was about to go to lunch. After that I'm meeting with a couple of builders. Maybe you could come back tomorrow."

"Why don't you let me handle this," Kane said, stepping forward slightly. He was not going to stand there and watch the man give Mel the runaround. He put both hands on the counter and leaned across it so that he was looking Homer Bledsoe right in the eye. "I'm only going to give you fifteen minutes to fill this order," he said. "And if I have to, I'll climb over this counter and personally assist you."

"Kane!" Mel's face flamed.

He ignored her. "Now what's it going to be?"

Homer's Adam's apple bobbed in his throat. Without taking his eyes off Kane, he reached for the telephone beside him. "I need a load of lumber," he said into the receiver. He read the list to the man on the other end. When he hung up, he looked at Mel. "You can pull around back, and they'll load it for you. I'll just send you a bill, if it's all the same to you."

"Thank you, Homer," Mel said politely.

Outside, she confronted Kane. "Did you have to do that?"

"Yes, I did. And I'll do it again the next time he forgets his manners."

Back at Abercrombie Grocery, Kane started work right away, measuring boards and cutting them with Wilton's electric saw. He was wet with sweat in no time at all. Finally, he stripped off his T-shirt and tied a red bandanna around his head. Mel, trying not to stare at the wide back that rippled with every move he made, played assistant, fetching what he needed. "You're very good at this," she said, noting how efficiently he worked, how he took time with even the smallest detail. "Why didn't you stick with it?"

He looked at her. "Prison got in the way."

She blushed. "Stupid question."

He smiled. "That's okay. Actually, I was taking a correspondence course in prison. Architecture. I didn't finish it."

He sounded disappointed. "Well, I know whatever you end up doing, you'll do it well." She walked away before she saw the expression on his face.

Kane watched her go. She was an amazing woman. He was further amazed that she could find so many good things about him when nobody else ever had.

Mel left shortly before noon to go home and prepare sandwiches. She discovered her sister still asleep. "Come on, Blair, you can't lie in bed all day," she said, shaking her sister awake. "You need to get up and eat something."

"I'm not hungry," the younger woman said sleepily. "Every time I eat I get sick."

"It's always like that in the beginning," Mel told her. "But it'll pass, and you'll feel better before long. Now come on into the kitchen. I'll make you something."

Blair started out of the room in her pajamas, then hesitated. "Where's the cutthroat?"

Mel gave an exasperated sigh. "Kane is working at the store, and he's not a cutthroat. Now what would you like for breakfast."

"Coffee and dry toast."

Mel went into the kitchen and headed straight for the refrigerator. Blair followed at a sluggish pace. "That's no kind of breakfast for an expectant mother," she said, wondering how Blair was going to take care of a baby when she couldn't take care of herself. She reached for a carton of eggs.

Blair shuddered when Mel put the plate of scrambled eggs and toast in front of her. "You'll feel better after you eat it," Mel promised, crossing the kitchen once more to start on the sandwiches she planned to take back. "And once you're finished eating, I want you to call Dr. Hadley for an appointment."

Blair looked startled. "What if he tells Daddy?"

"He can't discuss a patient with someone without that patient's approval. Besides, Daddy is bound to find out sooner or later."

"*I'm* not going to tell him," Blair said, taking a tiny bite of her eggs. "You'll have to do it."

Mel sighed. "Okay, I'll do it."

"How are you going to tell him?"

"I don't know yet. First let's get you to a doctor and make sure everything's okay."

"Does anybody else know?"

"Of course not. I wouldn't tell Kane without your permission."

Blair gave her a funny look. "I wasn't talking about Kane—I was talking about Harper."

Mel felt foolish. Of course one would assume she would confide in the man she'd been seeing for months instead of Kane, who'd only been there a few days. "Nobody knows," she said.

Blair bit into her toast and chewed. "No matter what, I don't want you to tell Daddy about the father being married and all."

Mel leveled her gaze at her sister. "You certainly don't have to worry about *that*," she said tersely. "I wouldn't think of telling him."

"You hate me now, don't you?"

Mel was weary of her questions. Sometimes her sister could be quite childish. "No, I don't hate you, Blair. I'm disappointed in you. I thought you would have used better judgment."

"Give it a rest, Mel. I didn't run a background check or have the guy tested for sexually transmitted diseases as I'm sure you would have done. I'm not you, and I never will be. *You've* always said and done the right thing. *You* always knew the answers to all the problems. Daddy listened to everything you said. He still does. He couldn't care less what I said."

"That's not true," Mel said, facing her sister once more. "You've always had center stage. You were the most popular girl in Hardeeville High."

"I was the *easiest* girl in Hardeeville High."

"Stop it." Mel's face flamed.

"Don't look so shocked, big sister. Besides, I'm sure you heard the rumors."

Mel stuffed the sandwiches into a sack with trembling fingers. Of course she'd known why her sister was so popular with the boys. But she hadn't wanted to admit it, because she would have to accept part of the blame. After all, she had practically raised Blair, despite being only a few years older.

"I don't know why you'd want to bring this up *now*," Mel said, feeling very close to tears.

"To show you how different we are and why I don't feel comfortable in my own house," Blair said. "The reason you get along with Daddy is because you're just like him. I'm more like Mama."

Mel's eyes glistened with unshed tears. "I'm surprised you even remember her," she said softly. "You were so young."

"Of course I remember her. She taught me to dance. She used to braid satin ribbons in my hair." Blair looked wistful. "And on cold mornings I would climb into the bed and snuggle with her until that old furnace warmed the house." Blair's eyes misted as well. She shoved her plate aside.

Mel went to her, taking both hands in hers and kneeling on one knee. "Blair, I'm so sorry. I tried so hard to make it up to you when she left, but I know it wasn't the same." She paused and swallowed. "I'll try very hard to be here for you now, okay? I'll drive you to the doctor myself when you get the appointment. Then, afterward, I'll take you shopping at the new mall in Pelzer. We can look for baby clothes, and maybe a couple of maternity outfits for you." She was talking so fast, she had to stop to catch her breath. Part of it was guilt, she suspected. Guilt because she knew precisely where to find their mother and hadn't divulged that information.

"I want to go lie down for a while," Blair said, looking suddenly weary. "Those eggs didn't sit well with me."

"You'll make that doctor's appointment?" Mel asked.

"After my nap," Blair told her, and disappeared down the hall.

"You're deep in thought this afternoon," Wilton said as Mel ate her sandwich in silence. "What's on your mind?"

Mel forced a smile she didn't feel. How could she answer truthfully and tell him what was going on with Blair? Wilton would be devastated at the thought of his unmarried daughter pregnant. "Nothing much," she said at last.

"She's missing the flower shop," Wilton told Kane. "I've never seen someone love her job as much as Mel. It's a shame she has to take off to help her old man clean up his store."

"I don't mind," Mel said. "Besides, Eunice is thrilled to be running the place."

Wilton opened his mouth to say something but closed it when Harper Beckwood pushed open the front door and stepped inside. "Harper, my boy, you're just in time for lunch," he called out in greeting.

"Good afternoon, Mr. Abercrombie," Harper said, nodding his head stiffly. Although Wilton had told him repeatedly to call him by his first name, Harper insisted on the formality. "Afternoon, Mel," he said. His gaze wandered to Kane, and a look of intense dislike crossed his face before he returned his attention to Mel. "I'd like to see you outside," he told her.

Mel nodded and stood, rewrapping her sandwich and placing it on the counter before making her way toward the door. She couldn't help but wonder what Harper had to say to her that couldn't be said in front of the others, then tossed him a worried look as she remembered his daughter. "Nothing's happened to Amy?" she said, following him outside.

"Amy's fine." Harper didn't say anything until they were outside. "I thought you said he was gone."

"You mean Kane? So that's what this is all about. Lord, Harper, news travels fast in this town."

"You told me he was gone, Mel. You lied."

"I didn't lie. He *was* gone, but I invited him to come back when he couldn't find a place to live. I was going to tell you Friday night when we went to dinner."

"Why, Mel?" Harper looked tired. "Why do you feel responsible for him? Why do you *insist* on making me look like a fool to the rest of this town?"

She was genuinely baffled. "How am I making you look like a fool?"

"Because we have an understanding between us, and you're spending all your time with this man. You've even opened your home to him. And he's not just any man, he's an ex-convict. I can't take it, Mel. I've tried to be patient with you, but you've gone too far this time."

"Harper, if you would only give Kane half a chance," she said, her tone pleading. "All he's doing is trying to make a fresh start in life. Come to dinner Sunday. Meet him for yourself."

He looked at her as if he thought she was crazy. "Are you suggesting I bring my eight-year-old daughter around a common criminal?" he said in disbelief.

"I'm going to pretend you didn't say that, Harper."

He crossed his arms and regarded her. "Maybe you need time to think about what you really want in life. Maybe it's not Amy and me after all."

"Don't drag Amy into this," she said. "I have no argument with her."

"She's my daughter, I have to bring her into it. She's grown very attached to you. She's already been hurt once. I don't want to see her hurt again."

Mel's heart sank at the thought of having her relationship with Amy altered in any way. At the same time she couldn't allow Harper to use Amy as a bargaining tool. "You're right, Harper, maybe I do need time to think," she said.

He looked surprised, then resigned. "Call me when you've come to your senses."

Mel watched him drive away, screeching his tires in a way that was totally out of character for him. Tears stung her eyes, but she was determined not to cry. If Harper thought he was going to force her to change a decision she felt was right, then he had a lot to learn about her. Still, it hurt to think that he might try to keep Amy from her.

The door to the store opened, and Kane hurried out. He took one look at her and knew it had to be bad. "Are you okay?"

She didn't trust herself to speak, so she nodded instead.

"He didn't hurt you?" he asked quickly. "If he so much as laid a hand on you—"

Mel looked at him. "Of course he didn't hurt me," she said. "Harper's not like that." She paused, noting the dangerous look in his eyes. "Besides, what would you have done, beat him up? Is that your solution to everything?"

Kane was suddenly angry. "It is if I catch a man hitting on a woman. You got a problem with that?"

"You can't solve the world's problems with your fists, Kane. Or by threatening people," she added, thinking of the scene with Homer Bledsoe.

Kane studied her for a moment, feeling stupid

now for charging out of the store to defend her. He'd never met anyone like her before. Having grown up with a father who was quick to raise his hand in anger, Kane didn't quite know how to take this gentle, giving creature who would never even think of striking another person. She had other ways of showing her displeasure—a cool look, a change in tone of voice—and they were as effective as his father's tactics had been.

He wished he knew how she did it.

"Is Harper upset because of me?" he asked at last.

"He's upset because I didn't do as he said," she responded, being deliberately vague.

"It'd be better if I left."

"No." Mel turned to him. The thought of him leaving bothered her more than she cared to admit. "I can't change who or what I am simply to make someone else happy, Kane. The sooner Harper realizes that, the better."

"I never meant to cause you trouble. You say the word, and I'm out of here."

She smiled, reached for his hand, and squeezed it. "I know. But then where would I be? Right now, you seem to be the only friend I have."

EIGHT

Several days later Mel arrived home to find Blair in the kitchen preparing a big tossed salad. The table had already been set and the hamburger meat molded into patties, ready to go under the broiler. "You must be feeling better," she said, noting Blair had dressed and put on makeup as well.

"I'm much better," she said. "I even made that doctor's appointment. He can see me next week."

"Good." Mel knew she should try to sound more enthusiastic. After all, that was a quick appointment. Nevertheless, she worried about Blair and the fact she felt so bad much of the time.

"Oh, and guess what? My agent called today. Have you heard of NuWave Wine Coolers?"

Mel shook her head. "Sorry."

"Well, the owner lives in Biloxi, and he's interested in finding someone from Mississippi to star in his commercials. They're holding auditions tomorrow afternoon, and I plan to be there."

"How are you going to get to Biloxi?" Mel asked. "You don't even own a car. Not only that, you don't drive."

"You'll have to drive me."

The way she said it, so matter-of-fact, annoyed Mel. But then, what else was new? Blair had always expected her to be there for her whenever she needed something. And she always had been. "I *can't* drive you. Daddy and I are painting shelves tomorrow. *And* I promised Amy I'd be at her recital. She asked me weeks ago."

"Don't you think *this* is a little more important than a child's dance recital?" Blair replied hotly.

Wilton picked that particular moment to walk through the back door with Kane on his heels. "What's going on?" he asked the minute he spied Blair's frowning face.

"Mel refuses to drive me to Biloxi so I can audition for a commercial," she said, shooting her sister an accusing look. "This could be my big chance."

"When do you have to be there?" Wilton asked.

"Tomorrow."

"That's pretty short notice," he said. He went to the kitchen sink and washed his hands. "I don't know, Blair. I don't like the idea of you girls on the highway all alone. What if Mel's car breaks down? How long will you need to stay?"

"I can come straight back after the audition."

"Hmm. That's a lot of driving. Not only that, Mel broke her glasses. She needs them when she gets behind the wheel. And she has that night-vision problem."

"Oh, for heaven's sake!" Blair said. "It's not as if I'm asking her to drive me to the other side of the country. Biloxi is only three hours from here."

Kane stepped forward. "I could drive her."

"You!" Blair gave a snort. "Now *there's* a thought."

Kane ignored her sarcastic reply and turned his attention to Wilton. "I used to drive eighteen-wheelers long distance," he said. "I have an excellent driving record."

"It's not your driving record I'm worried about," Blair said. "I'm more concerned with your prison record."

Kane fixed her with a fierce glare.

"Blair, that'll be enough!" Wilton said so loudly, they all jumped. "I will *not* have you talking to a guest in our house like that." He studied Kane for a moment. "It would be a big help to us, son, if you could do it. That way, me and Mel could get the shelves painted and be ready to start work on that area behind the meat case by the time you returned. You already know how to handle my old pickup truck."

The color drained from Blair's face. "Daddy, you can't mean that I'm going to have to ride all the way to Biloxi in your pickup truck with no air-conditioning."

"They can take my car," Mel said. "It'll be more comfortable."

Kane tossed her a smile. "I promise to be careful." Then, he turned to Blair. "If I hear one more peep out of you, I'm going to withdraw my offer and let you walk." The look on his face must've convinced the woman, because she didn't so much as utter a sound.

Kane and Blair left early the next morning. Mel packed sandwiches and a thermos of coffee and carried them out to the car, then pulled Blair aside for a moment. "Be sure to eat something," she said, having watched her get sick in the bathroom. Luckily, Wilton was still sleeping and had not heard her. "I'm sure you don't have a thing left in your stomach."

"I'll try." Blair hung her outfit in the backseat and stuffed her makeup case in the back as well. She planned to rent a room when she arrived in Biloxi so she could change clothes and make up her face for the audition. At the moment she looked rather pale.

"You ready?" Kane said, obviously anxious to get the whole thing over with. Neither of them had spoken to the other since the night before.

Blair nodded and got into the car without a word. She looked resigned. As Mel watched them ride off, she prayed Blair would be courteous toward Kane.

Mel and Wilton left for the store an hour later

and spent the entire day painting the shelves Kane had put in. "It looks pretty good," Mel said once they'd finished the job and started cleaning up. "We should be able to restock tomorrow."

Wilton nodded proudly. "I'm not going to let it get this bad again," he promised.

They arrived home shortly after five. Once Mel showered and scrubbed all the paint off, she prepared a light meal while Wilton cleaned up. "I have to be at Amy's dance recital at eight," she told her father as they finished up. "Would you like to come?" She knew how close her father was to Amy.

"Naw, I don't want to crowd you and Harper."

Mel didn't quite meet his gaze. "Harper and I won't be sitting together. In fact, he doesn't even know I'm coming."

Wilton looked surprised. "Did you two have a fight?"

"You might say we had a little misunderstanding. I'm sure it'll be okay, but I'm not going to let it stand in the way of this recital. I promised Amy two weeks ago I would be there."

"In that case I'll be happy to escort you," Wilton said.

The dance studio where Amy took ballet was buzzing with proud parents sitting on folding chairs along one wall. Mel, sitting with her father in the back row, managed to get several pictures of the dancers. When the recital was over and the children had received hearty applause, Amy rushed over to Mel and hugged her.

"I knew you'd come," she said. "Daddy said you couldn't make it, but I knew you wouldn't break your promise to me."

Harper, who'd been sitting in the front row, looked surprised to see Mel and her father. "I didn't see you come in," he said stiffly.

"You didn't actually think I'd miss Amy's first recital, did you?" she said, hoping to make him feel bad for even suggesting as much to his daughter.

"You're so busy with *other things* these days that I had no idea whether you'd find time."

"I always find time for the things that matter most to me," she said. Mel turned away from Harper and faced Amy. "I bought you a little something," she said, reaching into her purse for a slender box wrapped in pink paper. "To sort of celebrate your first recital."

Amy reached for the box eagerly. "May I open it now?"

"Certainly," Mel replied.

The girl tore the wrapping paper off and opened the box. "Look, Dad, a charm bracelet with a ballerina!" Amy threw herself against Mel and hugged her tightly. "Oh, thank you," she said. "I've always wanted one. Would you put it on for me?"

Mel handed Wilton her purse so she could put the bracelet on the girl's wrist. Once again, they hugged, and Mel was almost moved to tears by Amy's enthusiasm.

"Well, I guess we'd better be going," she said at last, wishing things weren't so tense between her and Harper.

"Don't tell me you're playing warden tonight," he said, leaning forward so he could whisper the words in her ear.

Mel felt her cheeks burn with anger, but she smiled for Amy's benefit. "Go to the devil, Harper," she said just as softly as she reached for Wilton's hand and led him out.

The telephone was ringing when they walked into the house twenty minutes later. Mel reached for it as she kicked off her heels.

"Is that you, Mel?" Kane asked from the other end of the line. "My God, I've been calling for almost two hours now."

"What's wrong?" she asked, noting the panic in his voice.

"It's Blair."

"What happened?" she said, automatically suspecting the worst.

"Just as we were loading up her bags to come home, she started having these pains and . . . bleeding real bad."

"Oh no," Mel said, and the words drew a frown

from Wilton, who was standing close by.

"I took her to the emergency room." He paused and took a deep breath. "I heard Blair tell them she was pregnant, and that the pains had been going on all day."

Mel sank onto the chair beside the telephone.

"What's wrong?" Wilton said. "Did something happen to Blair?"

Mel glanced up. "She's in the hospital, but she's going to be okay. I'll tell you in a minute." She turned her attention back to Kane. "Okay, give me the name and address of the hospital," she said. "We'll grab a change of clothes and be there in three hours."

Wilton was pacing the floor when she hung up. He stopped and regarded her. "What's going on, Melanie?" he asked, calling her by the name he used when he was upset.

"Just be patient, Daddy," she said. "I'll explain everything in the truck."

It was almost 1:00 A.M. when Wilton pulled into the parking lot of the hospital in Biloxi. "We made good time," he said, shutting off the engine.

Mel noted how weary he looked. He hadn't taken the news well. "Are you okay?" she asked softly.

He nodded, although he didn't quite meet her gaze. "I'm just angry right now," he said. "I'm wondering why the father of this baby isn't here to hold my daughter's hand through this bad time."

"Blair says it's over between them," Mel said, deciding a white lie was better than the truth in this case. "I think what Blair needs right now is the love and understanding of her family."

Wilton looked as though he would cry. "You're right. I'm sure Blair is feeling bad enough over what happened."

Mel held her father's hand as they walked into the emergency room. They found Kane right away. He looked relieved to see them. "She lost the baby," he said after a moment. "But the doctor assured me she's going to be all right."

"I want to see her," Wilton told them, looking very shaken over the news.

Although visiting hours had been over for quite some time, one of the nurses permitted Mel and Wilton inside Blair's room for a quick glance.

"She's sedated," the woman told them. "I don't expect she'll wake up till morning."

Once inside, a tearful Mel took her sister's hand in her own and squeezed it, wondering how Blair was going to cope with the loss of her child, wondering how she and her father would get through it as well. She gazed down at her sister, wishing she could take her in her arms and comfort her as she had when they were little girls. Much to her surprise, Blair opened her eyes.

"You came?" she said, her voice a mere whisper. "Is Daddy with you?"

"I'm right here, sugar," Wilton said, going around on the other side of the bed.

Blair closed her eyes. "I guess I don't have to keep it a secret any longer."

"I'm sorry, Blair," Mel said, leaning close. "Really sorry. But you'll be able to have more babies."

"The doctor says you can go home in a couple of days," Wilton told her, his eyes growing red again.

Blair didn't seem to be listening. "I don't want to think about it anymore," she said. "I want to go on with my life . . . as though none of it happened." She paused. "Did you hear the good news?" she said. "I was chosen to do the NuWave Wine Cooler commercial. So you see, the day wasn't totally shot." She closed her eyes and drifted off to sleep before she could see the stricken look on Mel's face.

When Mel and her father returned to the lobby, they found Kane waiting anxiously. "Everything okay?" he asked.

"She's fine," Mel told him. "We chatted with the nurse for a moment. It's just going to take a couple of days for her to get her strength back." Mel saw that Kane was holding a cup of coffee. "Is the cafeteria still open at this hour?"

"Naw, I got this in a vending machine down the hall. You want a cup?"

"Somebody is going to have to stay here for a couple of days," Mel told her father after they'd drunk their coffee. "Blair probably won't be released until tomorrow or the next day."

"I'll stay," Wilton said, "and bring her home when she's released."

"Are you sure? I certainly don't mind staying."

"No, you need to get back to those dogs of yours and everything else you've got going on, and Kane needs to get back to work at the store." He paused, and he looked sad for a moment. "Besides, I want to be here for Blair now. I feel as if I've let her down."

"None of this was your fault, Daddy," she told him. "Don't start blaming yourself."

Mel and Wilton rode back to the hospital in her car while Kane followed in the truck. Blair wasn't much better than she'd been the night before. "I hope I'm up and around by next week," she told Mel. "That's when they start shooting the commercial."

Mel simply couldn't understand how Blair could be worried about shooting a commercial when she'd just lost her baby. "Take care of yourself," she said as she left her room.

Mel and Kane were on their way an hour later, driving Wilton's pickup truck so he could bring Blair back in Mel's car. Mel didn't say anything for the first hour of the trip.

Finally, Kane glanced at her. "Why are you angry?"

Mel tried to hide her surprise. "What makes you think I'm angry?"

"You've got that look on your face. The same look you had right after your argument with Harper."

"I'm not angry, I'm disappointed."

"Okay, so how come?"

"It annoys me that Blair can worry about a stupid commercial when she's just lost her baby. I mean, not one word was said about that poor baby." Mel felt her eyes smart with tears as she said it. She wiped them away.

Kane reached over and squeezed her hand. "I don't think Blair's ready to be a mother. In fact, I'm not sure she'll ever be ready. Who knows, maybe she did the kid a favor."

Mel almost gasped out loud. "How can you say that?"

"Easy. Just 'cause people can have a baby doesn't mean they deserve one."

A look of tired sadness passed over her as she thought of the mother who'd abandoned them so many years earlier. She decided it was best to drop the subject.

It was shortly before noon when Kane pulled into the parking lot of a fast-food restaurant. "Are you hungry?" he asked.

She shrugged and looked out the window.

"Why didn't you tell Blair how you felt when you had the chance?"

"What Blair chooses to do with her life is none of my business."

"Yes, well, you're right about that."

She looked at him. "Whose side are you on?"

He made a show of holding both hands up as though surrendering. "I'm staying out of it. I figure the way I've screwed up my life, I have no right to tell anybody else how to live. Do you want a cheeseburger? If I remember correctly, there's a rest area not far from here. We can eat at one of the picnic tables. Do us good to get some fresh air after being in that hospital."

"That's fine with me."

"So, what do you want on your cheeseburger?"

"Ketchup."

"That's all?" He looked at her in disbelief. "You don't want lettuce, tomato, and onions?"

"Just ketchup."

"Wimp." He opened the door and climbed out, then made his way toward the restaurant, still shaking his head. He returned ten minutes later with two sacks. "I got you an order of fries," he said, joining her in the front seat once more. "I couldn't stand the thought of you eating that wimpy burger all by itself."

She smiled despite feeling heavyhearted. "I'm sorry I'm being such a stick-in-the-mud. I guess I really had my heart set on being an aunt."

"I know you did. I'm sorry."

Mel was surprised by the tenderness in his voice.

She would not have thought him capable of such an emotion a week and a half ago. "Here, let me hold the bags so you can drive," she said, taking them from him.

They remained silent as they rode the two miles to the rest area. They made their way to a group of picnic tables along the back of the park. Luckily, there wasn't anybody else around. Mel unpacked the bags. Kane's sandwich was considerably larger than hers. She chuckled. "I don't know how you're going to get your mouth around that."

"Trust me, I'll manage."

They concentrated on their lunch for a few minutes, with Kane proving he could indeed manage the big cheeseburger. He was the first to speak.

"Will Blair go back to New York once this is over?"

Mel nodded. "She always does."

"Do you mind?"

She pondered it. "I miss her when she's gone. We were so close after our mother left. But Blair isn't happy in Hardeeville, and she keeps Daddy and me tied in knots the whole time she's home. She wants bigger and better things. Like Mama did," she added.

Kane was surprised she'd brought up the woman. "Your mother didn't tell you she was leaving?"

Her face clouded. "No. We came home from school one day, and she was gone."

"I guess that really hurt."

She shrugged. "I don't remember. It was a long time ago."

He suspected she remembered very well. "What was she like?" he asked, attempting to find out more, wondering how much she'd tell.

"Very pretty. Blond, like Blair. She loved to read about far-off places. Like Paris and Spain and Germany. Said she wanted to go there one day. Who knows, maybe she got the chance after all."

He smiled. "I take it she wasn't your typical mother."

"She didn't bake cookies or volunteer as class mother, if that's what you mean. But she did preach good etiquette from a book she got out of the library. She said we'd need good manners and social skills if we ever got out of Hardeeville. She used to beg my father to sell the house and the store and move someplace like Atlanta. They fought about it all the time."

"Why do you think your father never remarried?"

She didn't hesitate. "I think he still loves my mother. He keeps her picture on his night table." She took another bite of her cheeseburger. "There's a lady down the road, a widow, who's been sweet on Daddy for years, but he won't give her the time of day." She saw that he had finished eating. "What are your parents like?"

He shrugged. "I don't know. I haven't seen them in fifteen years." When she looked surprised, he went on. "They used to fight all the time. My old man would get liquored up, come home, and beat the hell out of everybody. Us kids tried to get my mother to leave him, but she wouldn't."

The old hardness was back in his eyes. "Haven't you ever heard of Battered Woman's Syndrome?" Mel asked.

He wadded up his sandwich wrapper and empty fry carton and dropped them in the bag. "Yeah, I've heard of it," he said tersely, "but I've also heard of this thing called pride, and she had none. Far as I'm concerned, a woman lets a man beat on her, that's her business. But when she lets him beat on the kids, that's a crime for which they should both be punished."

Mel could see that he was close to anger, and she wondered if that anger was ever far from the surface. "How many children were there?"

"Five including me. Three boys and two girls. We all got the hell out of there as soon as we were old enough. My old man died ten years ago. The booze finally killed him. You ask me, the world's a better place because of it."

"And your mother?"

"Last I heard, she remarried. And you know what? This guy knocks her around too."

Mel didn't know what to say. It was obvious he was bitter about the whole thing. And why shouldn't he be? "I guess we'd better get back on the road," she said.

NINE

Mel and Kane arrived back in Hardeeville an hour later and, after changing into work clothes, headed for the store where they worked side by side until after six o'clock despite the fact it was Sunday.

"I've got an idea," Kane said, as he drove Wilton's truck home. "Instead of cooking, why don't we go out for something to eat? My treat," he added.

"Go out? Where?"

"Surely there's a decent restaurant in town. Besides, it's Sunday, and we deserve a break."

Mel thought of her Friday nights at Thelma's Restaurant that she'd enjoyed so much. Now that Harper was mad at her, it wasn't likely she'd be going anytime soon. "Yes, I know of a place," she said. "They serve a great chicken-fried steak."

When they arrived back at the house, Mel insisted Kane grab a shower first while she ironed one of his shirts from the duffel bag. It was the only time she could remember ironing for a man other than her father. Performing the little chore made her feel closer to him.

Kane stepped out of the bathroom freshly scrubbed and shaved and found the shirt hanging on the back of a kitchen chair. "Thanks," he said, appreciating the fact that she'd taken such care in ironing it when he was so used to wearing his clothes wrinkled. But tonight he wanted to look good. He didn't want to do anything that might embarrass her.

"You're welcome." Mel tried not to stare at the half-naked man before her with the magnificent chest. He was lean and brown without an extra ounce of fat on his body. She caught a whiff of him as he shrugged on the shirt. He smelled of soap and aftershave and male flesh. "Are you finished in the bathroom?" she asked, wanting to put some distance between them so she wouldn't gawk at him.

"It's all yours."

There was something decidedly intimate in stepping into the same bathtub Kane had stepped out of only moments before. His scent lingered in the mist that clung in the air and fogged the mirror over the sink. As Mel soaped herself, she felt her skin prickle at the thought of Kane using that same bar of soap across his broad chest. She pushed her thoughts aside.

Mel entered the kitchen thirty minutes later wearing a khaki skirt and a multicolored camp shirt. She was wearing her hair loose. "Now that's more like it," Kane said, noting she'd spent more time on her makeup as well.

Mel blushed. She had only worn her hair loose because it was still slightly damp, *not* because she'd been trying to seek his approval. At least that's what she'd told herself.

"Are you ready to go?" she asked. "I'm starved."

They made the twenty-minute trip to town in Wilton's truck. Thelma's was packed when they stepped inside. Mel blanched when she realized why. The evening service had just let out at the Hardeeville First Baptist Church.

"Oh no," she said aloud. "We can't eat here."

They were already inside. "What's wrong?" Kane said, glancing around the busy restaurant for a clue as to what was causing her distress. He didn't know if it was his imagination, but everybody seemed to be staring at them.

"I wasn't in church today," Mel whispered.

"Is that against the law in this town?"

"Of course not."

"It's me, isn't it?" he said, stiffening automatically. The thought of anyone mistreating her because of him made him mad as hell. "They're staring at you because you're with me, aren't they? Do you want to leave?"

"We can't just walk out. How would it look?"

"I don't give a flying fig *how* it looks. If you're uncomfortable—" He was interrupted when a matronly woman appeared out of nowhere.

"Hi, Mel. We missed you at church this morning. Would you like your usual table?"

"That will be fine, Vera," Mel said, taking Kane's hand in hers. He hesitated only a moment, then let her lead him to a table in the back.

Kane waited until they were alone before he said anything. "Your *usual* table?" he said, arching one dark brow.

"Harper and I used to come here on Friday night."

"And this is where you sat?"

"Yes. Do you mind?"

Hell yeah, he minded. "Should I?" he said instead, trying to play it cool.

He looked so handsome, it was hard to believe he was the same man who'd walked into Abercrombie Grocery wearing a straggly beard and filthy clothes. "No." She folded her hands in front of her. "If Harper and everybody else in this town chooses to misunderstand our relationship, that's their problem."

"Does he think we're romantically involved?"

"I have no idea what he thinks. But I can't base all my decisions on groundless suspicions."

Kane opened his menu and tried to concentrate, but he couldn't shake his feeling of disappointment over what Mel had said. Here he was, finding himself drawn more and more toward the woman, and she refused to think of him as anything more than a friend.

It scared him to think he might be falling for her. She was clearly not his type, not with her prim and proper ways. She had tied that glorious mass of hair up before she'd come into the restaurant, obviously trying to dispel any notion that she was attractive. But she *was* attractive, dammit, and he was having a hell of a time not noticing. He was also having a hard time not thinking about the times he'd kissed her.

"I highly recommend the chicken-fried steak."

"Huh?" Kane offered her a blank look.

Mel smiled. "You were a million miles away. What were you thinking?"

"You don't want to know."

He was scowling, and she didn't know why. "I don't?"

"Trust me on this one."

The waitress picked that particular moment to appear. Kane closed his menu. "We're both having the chicken-fried steak," he all but snapped.

They barely talked during the rest of the meal and on the way home. The silence was unbearable to Mel, who'd tried several times to start a conversation. She had made him angry, and she had no idea how or why. By the time he parked in front of the house, she was in a tizzy to find out what was bothering him. He opened her door and helped her out.

"Kane?"

"I'm going to check on the dogs," he said, then disappeared before she could say anything.

Mel went inside the empty house, kicked her shoes off, and called the hospital to check on Blair. Her father answered the phone and assured her Blair was okay and would be released the following day. Mel hung up and sat at the kitchen table, feeling depressed for reasons she didn't understand. Finally, she slipped her shoes back on and stepped out the back door.

The night air was cool; a full moon hung in the inky sky. She picked her way carefully across the backyard, using the floodlights from the house to light her way. She spied Kane stooped beside the Doberman they'd rescued a few days before.

"What are you doing?"

He glanced up at the sound of her voice. "I was just checking on Rover."

"Rover?" She chuckled softly. "That's not a very original name." When he merely shrugged, she went on. "Kane, have I said or done anything to make you angry?"

He stood and faced her squarely. "Yes, you have, Mel, although I doubt you'd ever do anything intentionally to hurt a person."

"Are you angry with me because we sat at the table Harper and I usually use?"

"I'm not mad because we sat there. I guess I'm hurt that it didn't seem to make any difference to you when it made a helluva lot of difference to me."

"What do you mean?"

He stepped closer and placed his hands on his hips, then stared at her for a full minute in the darkness. She was truly lovely, but he was certain she wasn't aware of that fact. He took a deep breath. "I'm damn sick and tired of your thinking of me as just some charity case."

"I don't think of you as a charity case."

"How can you not? Here I am, no job, no place to live, and less than two hundred bucks to my name."

"You *do* have a place to live. And sooner or later one of those interviews is going to pay off, and you're going to land a good job."

He was touched that she believed in him, and it strengthened his determination. "That's not really what this is about," he said. "I know I'm going to succeed because I refuse to give up. This is about you and me. I want you, Melanie Abercrombie, and you're too damned blind to see it."

She took a step back.

He took two forward.

"You can back up clear to the hog pen," he said, "but I'm not going to let you get away until you've heard me out."

"I'm listening," she told him, when every instinct in her body warned her they were moving in a dangerous direction. She should turn and run as fast as she could to the house. Yet his gaze dared her to budge. "What is it you want to say to me?"

"I want to know how you feel about me."

Mel took a deep breath. "That's easy. I think you're very nice and—"

"Cut the crap, Mel, I mean do you like me the way a woman's *supposed* to like a man?"

When Mel didn't answer, he reached up, cupped the back of her head in his hand, and pulled her to him, planting his mouth across hers. He kissed her hard, savagely.

He released her without warning. Mel stumbled. "What was *that* all about?" she demanded through bruised lips.

"I have to know how you feel," he said matter-of-factly. "I can't hang around this place, seeing you and wanting you when you don't even take me seriously." He paused and took a shaky breath. Her eyes were luminous in the moonlight, her mouth wet from his kiss.

"How do you think I feel, Kane?" she said, her emotions suddenly getting the best of her. "What woman wouldn't be flattered by the things you say? But this is happening too fast. I don't know if it's right." Her eyes filled with tears as she thought of her sister lying in a hospital, and of her father sitting next to her, feeling guilty and wondering where he'd gone wrong. She thought of Harper, who was angry with her for opening her doors to an ex-con and a man she'd come to care about in a short time. Finally, she thought of Amy, an eight-year-old who needed her friendship more than ever.

A sob escaped Mel's lips. "I just don't know what's right anymore."

Kane's heart turned over in his chest at the sight of her tears. "Oh, baby," he said, taking her in his arms. "I'm sorry for making you cry."

Mel snuggled against him, taking great comfort in his warmth and strength. "You didn't make me cry," she said, her words muffled against his chest. "I'm worried about other things. I can't stop thinking there's something I should have said to Blair. Maybe I've judged her too harshly. And Daddy, sitting there blaming himself for everything. I should have stayed."

He stroked her hair as she talked. "I've never met anyone like you," he said. "You're so devoted to those you love." At the same time he wondered if she would ever take time for her own happiness.

Finally, when her tears were spent, Mel raised her head and studied him in the moonlight. He was so handsome. Much too handsome for a simple farm girl who'd never been more than two hundred miles from home. But she was drawn to him regardless, and she knew her feelings had little to do with reason.

"I want you, too, Kane," she said suddenly, surprising them both with her honesty. But that's the only way she knew how to be. "You do things to me that no other man has." She blushed as she said it. "I feel as if I've known you all my life."

Kane kissed her softly, and Mel parted her lips so he could taste the inside of her mouth. She kissed him back with a hunger she'd never known. The kiss echoed through her thoughts, sang through her heart. She felt drugged. He pulled away, leaving her mouth burning and yearning at the same time.

"I want to make love to you, Mel," he whispered against her open lips.

Her heart leaped to her throat. The thought sent a shiver of anticipation through her and at the same time frightened her. "I can't," she said. "I could get pregnant. Just like Blair."

His gut clenched at the thought of doing anything that might hurt her. "Let me just hold you . . . and feel you next to me," he said.

She hesitated.

"Do you trust me?"

"Of course I do."

"I mean, really?"

She thought about it. He looked so sincere, it was hard not to trust him, even though she was accustomed to doubting and second-guessing everything he said to her. Had she spent too much time listening to Eunice? "Yes, really," she said, deciding it was the truth.

"Let's go inside." He took her hand and led her up

the back stairs and into the house. Still holding hands, they walked down the hall toward her bedroom.

Mel didn't say anything until he'd laid her down on the bed. "Kane, I think we should talk," she said.

He lay down beside her and gathered her in his arms. It felt so good, so *right*, being there with her. "What do you want to talk about?"

She hesitated. "I know we're not going to make love, but I have to tell you just the same, I've never been with a man."

"Not even Harper?"

"I told him I wasn't ready."

Kane kissed her forehead and simply held her against him for a time. He felt an unexpected wave of tenderness wash through him. Prison had not destroyed all his emotions as he'd once thought. "I won't do anything to put you at risk, Mel," he said softly. "No matter how badly I want to be inside you." He shifted on the bed and raised up on one elbow. "But I would like to look at you . . . and touch you."

She gazed back at him, feeling very vulnerable but thinking she'd never felt so close to another human as she did at that moment. He reached for the buttons on her blouse, and she stilled his hands. "Would you turn off the light?"

He gazed down at her. "How about I leave on the light in your closet? Would that be okay?"

She nodded, and he got up from the bed. When

he returned, the room was dim, with only a bit of golden light peeking out from the closet.

"Better?" She nodded, and Kane reached for the clasp in her hair. He undid it, then fanned her hair out on the pillow. It was thick and heavy but silky to touch. "Beautiful," he said. "I wish you'd wear it down always."

He kissed her again, this time softly and lingeringly, simply enjoying the taste and texture of her lips. He drank in her sweetness, stroking her cheek with one hand, marveling at the feel. He had forgotten how soft skin could be, how smooth. He'd forgotten how good a woman could smell. Mel smelled like wildflowers and bath soap. Prison had smelled of unwashed bodies and cigarette smoke. Of sweat and blood. He blocked the thoughts. Nothing was going to infringe on this time right here and now.

He unbuttoned her blouse slowly, then opened it. He fingered her white lace bra, noting how delicate it was, how utterly feminine. Kissing her again, he eased the cups aside. At first he thought he'd died and gone to heaven. It was too much to comprehend, this lovely shy woman so willing to let this love-starved man touch her. He reached for her again, crushing her to him as he pressed his lips against hers.

Mel returned the kiss with what she decided could only be described as reckless abandon. All her inhibitions vanished into thin air as his mouth caressed hers, coaxing a response that surprised her as much as it delighted him. Kane broke the kiss, and his mouth reappeared at her throat. He moved a hand to her breast, and she closed her eyes as he fondled it and teased the nipple to erectness. Her stomach fluttered at the intimacy of his touch. She drank in the sensations, then moaned softly when they became too much.

He moved his hands under her skirt and skimmed her hips and thighs with a wide palm. He felt her stiffen slightly. "It's okay," he whispered.

Mel bit her bottom lip to keep from crying out when his hand moved around to her belly. It felt too good, too sweet. Something inside leaped to life. Instinctively, she arched against him.

"Feel good?"

"Yes." It came out sounding like a hoarse croak.

Suddenly, his hand was inside her panties, caressing, teasing, sending jolts of excitement through her. Fully aroused, Mel parted her thighs. Kane stroked her until she thought she'd burst from the pleasure of it. Finally, he touched her, seeking the small bud that was giving her such a fit at the moment. He flicked it softly with deft fingers, then dipped one finger inside where she was already wet.

"You're so sexy," he whispered, stroking her as he talked. His own arousal was causing him a great deal of pain.

Mel tried to lie still on the bed as he worked his magic. She was on fire. He touched her again, and she sucked her breath in sharply, afraid to give in to the wondrous sensations. She was at the edge, the breaking point, and the thought that she might lose control frightened her.

"It's okay, baby," Kane said, realizing he, too, was at the point of no return and about to do something he hadn't done since he was a teenager. "Just relax and enjoy it," he managed before the pleasure became too great.

Desire hit Mel, swift as a lightning bolt, shattering the cool reserve that had taken a lifetime to construct. She cried out as she rose to meet a moment of giddy, uncontrolled passion. She trembled and shook, clinging to Kane as though he were a lifeline and she a drowning woman. The release brought tears to her eyes, and for a moment she forgot about everything else except the man beside her.

Finally, as she coasted back to reality, she knew she would never be the same.

TEN

Very gently, Kane pulled her skirt back into place and took her in his arms, having enjoyed the touching and kissing as much as she. Although they had not actually made love, the simple act had restored some part of him. He was relieved that he was capable of giving without taking. He gazed down at her, thinking she had never looked lovelier or more desirable.

It was then he noticed her eyes were wet with tears. "I'm sorry," he whispered, his tone regretful. "I made you cry again."

Mel snuggled against him, feeling very foolish for the tears. "I'm not crying because I'm sorry for what we did," she said. "I'm crying because it was so wonderful. Is it always that good?"

He smiled tenderly, at the same time wondering how she'd managed to go thirty years without experiencing sexual intercourse. He'd been fourteen the first time. "It's good if you care about the person you're with," he answered at last, loving the feel of her against him. She probably didn't have a clue how excited he got from just touching her. He could already feel himself becoming aroused again.

She was thoughtful for a moment. "Thank you for not pushing me, Kane," she said.

"I knew you weren't ready. Besides, I'd rather our first time be perfect."

"*Our* first time?"

"You heard me right," he said, then tightened his arm around her possessively. "After tonight, I'm going to insist I'm the one."

She raised up and tossed him a saucy smile, which wasn't easy for a girl who'd never flirted in her life. "Making demands already, are we?"

He grabbed her shoulders and pulled her on top of him so that she was forced to acknowledge how hard he was. Her smile faded, and he knew he'd managed to convey that fact. "Damn right." He kissed her hungrily.

Mel was the first to pull away. She gazed into his black eyes and was made anxious by the intensity of his look. She was falling head over heels in love with him. If they *did* make love, how would she ever be able to let him go when the time came? "This is all happening too fast for me," she said. "Tonight was wonderful and all, but I need more time."

"Does this have anything to do with Harper?"

It would have been a whole lot easier to let him think her reluctance was based on her relationship with Harper instead of letting him know what a coward she was. She simply didn't want to be hurt. Hadn't Eunice warned her time and again of the dangers of falling in love? Hadn't she witnessed firsthand her father's pain when her mother had left?

"Harper and I have been friends for a long time, Kane," she said, being deliberately vague simply because she had no answers at the moment. "I'm very fond of his little girl. You can't expect me to turn my back on them."

"I don't care how many *friends* you've got. I just don't want him to be your lover."

"Besides," she added, as if she hadn't heard him, "how do I know you're going to stay in Hardeeville? How do I know you won't get bored to death in another week and take off?" She held her breath for his reply.

"Is that what you're afraid of?"

"It has crossed my mind. Suppose you don't find a job here?"

"You ask a lot of questions, Mel. I don't have all the answers right now."

Mel eased off the bed. Of course, he had no way of knowing whether he'd find a decent job in Hardeeville or if he'd be forced to move on.

"Where are you going?"

"I have work to do. Daddy and Blair will be back tomorrow. I want to get the place in order."

He raised up and reached for her. "I'll help you. What do you want me to do?"

She pulled away. "Kane—" She took a deep breath. "We need to back off a little. Let's not rush into anything right now."

That was not the answer he'd expected after what they'd just shared. All the light went out of his eyes, and when he spoke, his voice was flat and emotionless. "Why? Are you ashamed to have folks think you're involved with an ex-con?"

Her face flamed. "Not at all." She was too embarrassed to tell him the truth, that she was afraid he'd leave and she'd end up looking like a fool. Poor old Melanie Abercrombie, so afraid of being an old maid that she jumped on the first man who ever looked at her. Then, in her desperation, she chased him right out of town.

Kane saw the doubt in her eyes and released her. She was already chastising herself for what she'd done. "Don't worry, I won't say anything," he said. He got off the bed and left the room without another word.

Kane was awakened the next morning by someone knocking at the front door. He peeked out of the window and saw a sheriff's car parked out front. He froze, then grabbed his jeans and stepped into them. He hurried into the hall and found Mel coming out of her own room in her bathrobe.

"It's the Sheriff's Department," he said in a low voice. "What do you think they want?"

"I haven't the foggiest idea," she said, trying to rub the sleep out of her eyes as she started for the stairs. "That's what I'm about to find out."

"Wait!" Kane grabbed her by the arm and almost shoved her against the wall. "What if they're here for me?"

"For you? Why would they be here for you?"

He tried to think. Cops made him nervous, always had. He'd been dodging them all his life. "Maybe they've discovered they didn't have enough evidence to let me go. Maybe they've changed their minds." The thought of going to prison made his blood run cold, made him want to run.

Mel shrugged free. "Kane, would you settle down, for heaven's sake! Has it not occurred to you they may have another reason for being here?" Panic filled her eyes. "Oh no, what if something's happened to Blair or Daddy? What if it's bad news?"

She raced down the stairs, unlocked the front door, and threw it open. The heavyset uniformed man on the other side took off his hat.

"Oh, Sheriff Clancy, what brings you here this morning?" she said breathlessly.

The sheriff opened his mouth to speak, then paused when he saw Kane come up behind Mel. He stared for about thirty seconds before Mel realized what he was looking at. "Oh, this is Mr. Stoddard, Sheriff. He's staying with us for a while."

The man nodded. "Is Wilton here?"

"No, Daddy's out of town. He should be back this afternoon. Is anything wrong?"

"Did you know his hog has done broke out of the fence again?"

"Pork Chop is loose?"

"Yeah. The Widow Barker called and said her sow was in heat. That hog o' yours is tryin' to tear down the pen."

"I'll go right away, Sheriff." Mel turned to Kane. "Would you mind coming with me?"

"Sure, let me grab a shirt."

"I'm sorry I had to rouse you outta bed, Mel," Sheriff Clancy said, as soon as she managed to get the hog away from Mrs. Barker's house. "Old lady Barker was madder than a hornet when she called me this morning. Told me she was going to shoot him."

"It's okay, Sheriff. Daddy should have fixed that pen once and for all, but you know how he puts things off."

The sheriff nodded, then turned to Kane, who followed behind the hog and nudged him every so often to keep him moving. "So how do you like our town, Mr. Stoddard?" he said.

Kane met the man's gaze. His look was one of distrust, as though he expected the sheriff to put handcuffs on him and toss him in the back of the car any minute. "I like it okay," he said at last. "Just want to find a job and a place to live."

"Kane is staying at our place while he remodels the store. He's an excellent carpenter, if you know of anybody who's looking."

"I'll keep that in mind," Sheriff Clancy said. He checked his wristwatch. "Well, I'd best get back to the office. Ya'll let me know if you need any help fixin' that pen."

"Thanks, Sheriff." Mel smiled and watched him drive off.

Mel tugged on the rope, and the hog merely looked at her as though she'd lost her mind. "Don't go getting stubborn on me," she warned.

"Here, let me take the rope," Kane offered. "I'll help you get him home, then come back for the truck." He tugged the rope several times, and the hog started moving. "See, you have to be firm and let him know who's in charge," he told her. He noted her shapely legs in a pair of cotton shorts that she wouldn't have thought of wearing to town. In her haste to dress, she hadn't bothered with a bra. Her nipples were erect beneath the flimsy T-shirt she wore. His gut clenched with desire as he remembered taking each one between his lips the night before. He grinned suddenly. "But you're just a girl, I don't expect you to be able to do it."

A humorous smile touched her lips. "Oh, is that right? Are you calling me a sissy?"

"Yep, that's what you are, a bona fide sissy."

"Kane, I could get this hog back *without* a rope, if I wanted to. I could *talk* him into following me home. Women don't need a bunch of muscles when they've got brains. Men, on the other hand—"

"Since when do you have anything against muscles?" he interrupted. "Seems to me you've been looking at mine a lot lately."

Mel blushed. "I have *not* been looking at your muscles."

"Oh yes, you have. Last night when I came into the kitchen to get the shirt you'd ironed for me, I thought your eyeballs would pop right out of your head."

The blush spread clear to the tips of her ears. So he had noticed her staring.

Kane laughed out loud at her red face. "You're beautiful when you do that, you know it? Even prettier than last night when you—" He let the sentence drop, but he was certain Mel knew he was referring to what had happened in her bedroom. Kane stopped walking, and the hog stopped and looked up as though to tell him to make up his mind. "I'm sorry we argued."

Mel came to a halt as well. She met his gaze. "I'm sorry too," she said.

They stared at each other for a moment. Finally, Kane reached up and cupped her cheek. "I shouldn't have tried to rush you into something. We both know I've got to get my life together before I can make any promises. I lost my head."

"So did I," she said, thinking of how they'd spent a portion of the evening. She'd gotten very little sleep worrying about it.

"Then we can go back to being best friends?" he asked.

It occurred to her at that moment that that's exactly what they were. Best friends. She trusted him with her life. She'd already trusted him more than she had any other man.

"Best friends," she said.

Kane leaned forward slightly and brushed his lips across hers. When he pulled away, he was smiling. "I guess we'd better get this slab of bacon home."

They started down the street once more with the hog behind them. Mel realized she had never felt happier.

Mel spent the day cleaning and restocking the shelves Kane had built while he worked in the meat area, building cabinets for storage. The place was really beginning to take shape, she decided. Once she was finished with the shelves, she grabbed a ladder and began cleaning the paneling. Years of dust and grime and tobacco smoke were wiped away, leaving the wood shiny and smelling of lemon oil.

"Look how dirty we are," Mel said when they climbed into the truck and headed home.

Kane reached over and wiped a smudge from her nose. "It feels good to put in an honest day's work, though, doesn't it?"

"Have you always been a hard worker?" she asked, amazed that he could go for hours without a break. She'd also discovered he was somewhat of a perfectionist. He didn't walk away from a task until it was completed just so.

"I pulled a lot of overtime at the print shop in prison," he said. "Just to keep from having to go back to my cell. Then I studied. It helped pass the hours. Otherwise, I'd have spent all my time staring at four walls and feeling sorry for myself."

Her car was parked in the driveway when they pulled in front of the house at six o'clock. Wilton had called after lunch to let them know he and Blair had arrived home safely. They found him sitting in the living room with the newspaper.

"How's Blair?" Mel asked.

"Tired and sore. The doctor told her to stay off her feet for a couple of days. She's sleeping right now." He paused and chuckled. "What dumpster did you two crawl out of?"

Mel laughed as well. "I'll admit we look pretty bad. Kane, you want the shower first?"

"No, you go ahead. I'll have a cold drink with your dad while you clean up."

Mel started down the hall, then paused long enough to look in on her sister. Sure enough, Blair was sleeping soundly. She closed the door softly and made for the bathroom.

Blair appeared in her nightgown while they were finishing up dinner. Kane jumped up and offered her his chair. "I'm not eating," she said. "I just came in for something cold to drink."

Mel got up quickly. "You could have called me to get it for you," she said, going straight to the refrigerator for the tea pitcher. She pulled an ice tray from the freezer. "How do you feel?"

"Tired."

"You really should eat something, you know. You're not going to get your strength back unless you do."

"I can't afford to gain even an ounce right now," Blair replied as she took a sip of the iced tea. "I have to leave for Biloxi tomorrow evening."

"You can't be serious," Mel said. "You just got out of the hospital."

Blair's eyes took on a hard look. "I'm dead serious. This could be my big chance."

"How can you even think of doing a commercial at a time like this?" Mel asked, forgetting for the moment they had an audience. "You just lost your baby."

"What am I supposed to do, Mel? Wear sackcloth and rub ashes on my face? It's over. And a good thing too. Can you imagine *me* with a baby?"

Mel gasped out loud. "How can you say that!"

"That's enough, girls," Wilton said.

Blair ignored him and slammed her glass on the counter. "Stop trying to act like my mother, Mel. That's all you've done my entire life. You're nothing like her. My mother was pretty and alive. You're a dried-up old maid whose only ambition in life is to marry Harper Beckwood and have a dozen brats. Really, Mel, why don't you just slit your throat and be done with it?"

Wilton shoved his chair from the table and stood. "I said that's enough." He glared at Blair. "I don't ever want to hear you talk to your sister like that. She all but raised you, you know."

Blair's eyes teared. "So I've been told over and over again," she said, wiping them away. "She cooks, she cleans, she works sixteen hours a day. The poor Widow Barker doesn't stand a chance with you. And neither does Mama."

"What's *that* supposed to mean?" Wilton demanded.

"Excuse me, I think I'll leave the three of you alone to work this out," Kane said, feeling uncomfortable with the family argument. Nobody seemed to notice when he let himself out the back door.

"I asked you a question, young lady," Wilton said.

"Daddy, you know Mrs. Barker is hot on your path," Blair said. "Don't be so naive."

"What's that got to do with your mother?"

"Mama's been writing to us for months now, but Mel hides the letters before we can see them."

Wilton looked stricken. He glanced at Mel, who had remained quiet throughout the conversation. She looked away as though she couldn't bear to look at him. He turned his attention back to Blair. "How do you know this?"

Blair shifted nervously. "I found the letters hidden in her lingerie drawer."

He arched two bushy brows. "I don't suppose you want to tell me why you were going through your sister's belongings in the first place."

"I was looking to borrow a pair of panty hose, that's all. You don't actually think I'd wear anything *she* has."

Wilton sank onto a chair and wiped his forehead with a napkin. He looked weary. "Why do you have to make trouble every time you come?" he asked Blair. "You blow through town once a year, and all you do is stir things up."

"Maybe I'm checking to see if you and Mel are alive and kicking under all that dust."

"Our lot in life ain't so bad. I haven't heard any complaints from Mel." He glanced at his oldest, who offered him a slight smile.

"It's not in her to complain. She'll stay in this house and take care of you till you both rot."

"She's going to marry Harper."

Blair gave a snort and regarded her sister. "She's not in love with Harper." Fresh tears filled her eyes. "She's in love with Kane."

"That's enough, Blair," Mel choked out, her face on fire. "You have no right to say such things."

Wilton stood once more. "You'd best go back to bed," he told his youngest. "You just got out of the hospital. You don't need to tire yourself."

Blair picked up her iced tea and started for the door. Mel followed.

"Not so fast, Melanie," Wilton said. "You and I are going to have a little talk."

Blair tossed a triumphant smile her sister's way before she disappeared down the hall.

ELEVEN

The bar beckoned to him with neon lights promising pool tables, poker machines, and the coldest beer in town. Kane pulled off the main road and parked his motorcycle. He couldn't remember the last time he'd enjoyed a cold beer. Certainly not in the last three years.

A wall of cigarette smoke hit him as he walked into the Wayside Tavern. It was a poor sight inside: concrete floor, battered tables, and fake leather chairs with the stuffing spilling out in places. A badly scuffed bar ran the length of one wall.

Several people stopped what they were doing and stared as he crossed the room and grabbed a barstool.

A plump middle-aged woman with frosted hair and a too-tight skirt ambled his way. "Well, hello there, Tall, Dark, and Handsome. What can I get you?"

Kane pulled his wallet out of his back pocket and offered her a polite smile. "Whatever you have on draft is fine."

She grabbed a cold glass from a cooler and filled it. "That'll be one twenty-five," she said, putting it in front of him.

He handed her the money plus a tip, then stood and carried his drink to the back where the pool tables were. Various games skirted the room. He dropped two quarters in one of the pinball machines, and it came to life. He was on his second game before he realized someone was watching him.

"You're pretty good at that," a tall, angular man said.

Kane continued to play in silence.

"I ain't seen you in here before. You must be new in town."

"Yeah."

"Where you from?"

Kane didn't bat an eye. "Leavenworth Prison."

"No kiddin'?" He looked impressed. "What brings you to Hardeeville?"

"You ask a lot of questions."

He held up his hands as though surrendering. "Hey, I'm just being friendly, that's all. You don't want no company, just tell me to get lost."

Kane turned fully around and offered his hand. "Name's Kane Stoddard. I thought I'd try to find me a job here."

The man shook his hand. "I'm Harry. What kind of work you lookin' for?"

Kane noticed he smelled and wondered when he'd last bathed. "Whatever's paying."

"Good luck. I been out of work since last fall."

"You don't say." Kane wondered how hard he was trying. He hadn't shaved in probably a week, and his clothes looked dirty. He wouldn't make much of an impression in an interview.

"So where d'you live?"

"I'm staying with the Abercrombies until I find a place."

"You mean Wilton Abercrombie and his daughters?" the man said in disbelief. He let out a low whistle. "Oh, man! I know all about the Abercrombie girls!"

"Yeah?"

"Yeah." He leaned closer and whispered right in Kane's face. "I hear tell the youngest one will let anybody in her britches, but the older one won't so much as let a man get near her. Everybody knows Harper Beckwood's been trying these past few months."

Kane's arm shot out before he even had time to consider what he was doing. He grabbed the man up by the collar and jerked him close. "I'd appreciate it if you'd kindly refrain from saying anything bad about the Abercrombies," he said. "Especially Melanie Abercrombie."

The man swallowed nervously. Several others

paused at the pool tables and stared. "Hey, man, I didn't mean nothin' bad by it. Everybody in town thinks the world of that family." Kane released him, and he adjusted his collar. "I just cain't figure out what a guy like you is doing there," he went on. "Nothing personal, but—"

"You saying I'm not good enough?"

"No, no, I'm thinking you got to be bored outta your mind there." The man gave him a nervous smile. "C'mon and let me buy you a drink. You look like you need to relax and have a little fun. You're all wound up."

Kane drained his glass and followed Harry to the bar, where it was promptly refilled. He *was* all wound up, had been since he'd laid eyes on Mel.

Harry took a long drink of his whiskey and wiped his mouth on the back of his hand. He chanced a look in Kane's direction. "So what were you in for?"

Kane decided he was desperate for a friend. "I killed a man with my bare hands," he said. "For asking too many questions."

Harry paled before his eyes. Just then a woman sat on the other side of Kane and asked him for a light. Harry handed him a pack of matches. "I'm going back to play pool so you can talk to the lady," he said, as though anxious to escape.

Kane turned in the woman's direction and lit her cigarette. Her nails were long and red as fresh blood. She inhaled deeply and mumbled a word of thanks.

"So what's your name, stranger?" she asked in a voice that was soft and fuzzy around the edges, suggesting this wasn't her first drink of the day.

"Kane Stoddard." She was attractive, with thick chestnut hair and lips the color of cinnamon sticks. On closer inspection he noted faint lines near her eyes and mouth that told him she wasn't as young as she appeared at first glance.

"Mine's Bitty. You live around here?"

Kane nodded but didn't offer any information. "I'm new in town."

"I thought so. I would'a remembered you." She took in the length of him, then finished her drink in one clean gulp. "You wanna dance?"

Kane glanced around the tavern. There wasn't a jukebox in sight. "I don't hear any music."

"There's music at my place," she said.

He arched one dark brow. "Oh yeah? What kind of music?"

"I got anything you want, honey."

It was almost too easy. Kane stood. "I wish I could, Bitty, but I've got somewhere I'm supposed to be. Maybe another time." He walked out the door without a backward glance.

It was after midnight when Kane walked into the back door of the Abercrombie house and found Wilton sitting at the kitchen table with a glass of milk. "My stomach was acting up," the older man confessed. "You want a glass?"

"Don't mind if I do." Kane made his way to the refrigerator for the milk.

"So how was your evening?" Wilton asked once Kane joined him at the table.

"I played pinball at the Wayside Tavern."

"What'd you think of the place?"

Kane was thoughtful. "I think it's kinda sad." He thought of Bitty, how tempted he'd been to go home with her a split second before common sense had kicked in. He'd ended up taking a long ride on his motorcycle.

"I had a talk with my daughters tonight," Wilton said, changing the subject. "Blair seems to think there's something going on between you and Mel."

Kane froze, the milk glass poised halfway to his mouth. He put it down. "Mr. Abercrombie, I want you to know right now that I have in no way jeopardized your daughter."

"That's not what I'm asking you, son. I want to know how you feel about her. Are you in love with Mel?"

Kane pondered it. "Maybe I am. I care for her an awful lot." It was the only excuse he could think of for not going off with Bitty when he had the chance. Lord knew, his body was eager. But for once in his life, he knew who and what he wanted, and it wasn't a one-night stand from a woman he'd met in a sleazy bar. Only problem was, he didn't know how to go about *getting* what he wanted. In the past he'd simply taken it. This time he wanted to do it right.

"Do you think she has fallen in love with you?" Wilton asked.

"I wish I knew." Kane sighed heavily. "I'm not really in a position to make any demands on Mel," he said. "I have nothing to offer her."

"You have yourself." He studied Kane's forlorn expression. "You don't think that's enough, is that it?"

"Something like that, yeah." He paused. "I was working toward a degree in prison, but I still have a ways to go."

"How far?"

"Another year and a half. Maybe longer."

"So what's the problem? There's a four-year college in Pelzer, not more than twenty-five miles from here."

Kane shrugged. "I'd be thirty-two or three by the time I graduated."

"You're going to be that age anyway. Wouldn't it be nice to have your degree by that time?" When Kane didn't answer, he went on. "If you applied now, you could be accepted by fall. What's stopping you?"

Kane's face clouded. "All I want to do is get my life together right now. In prison I had nothing better to do with my time than work on a degree. It sort of kept me going. Now I want to find a job and get a place to live."

"I don't want you to move out, Kane," the man said. "If there's a chance my daughter has found the man she wants to spend her life with, I want him close by."

"I'm an ex-con, Mr. Abercrombie. Harper Beckwood would make a better husband." It galled him to say it, but he knew it was true.

"You're the most honest man I know, Kane. As I see it, my daughter would be lucky to have you."

Kane took a sip of his milk. He couldn't remember when anyone had ever said anything nicer to him.

Wilton and Blair left for Biloxi the next morning. Mel could see that her father was in no mood to drive the girl, but Blair wasn't about to let him out of it. Mel wondered if he was still mad at her for hiding the letters Adelle had written. She'd tried to explain *why* she'd hidden them—that she didn't want her mother hurting them any more, but he insisted on seeing the letters anyway. He'd spent the rest of the evening in his room with the door closed, while Mel had stayed in hers feeling guilty. She realized she'd had no right to keep the letters from him.

Now he looked tired and preoccupied. "I'm ready

for Blair to go back to New York," he whispered to Mel before he pulled out of the driveway in her car. "She's driving me crazy."

"Don't worry about a thing here, Daddy," Mel told him, her eyes pleading for forgiveness. "We should have most of the store finished up by the time you get back tomorrow."

It was obvious Petals-n-Things was having a slow morning as Mel walked through the front door. She found Eunice sipping coffee and reading a tabloid boasting a new diet on the front page that promised a twenty-five-pound weight loss in fourteen days. The headlines also stated that Elvis was indeed alive and living in Spokane.

Eunice looked surprised to see her. "Well, hello, stranger. I was beginning to think you'd forgotten all about me."

Mel leaned against the counter and regarded her with a quizzical look. "Last time I was here, you accused me of being neurotic about this place and told me to leave."

"Yeah, but that's before I heard there was a new man in your life. Word has it he's spent time behind bars. Imagine my surprise when I heard. Here we are, practically best friends, and you didn't even tell me."

Mel didn't miss the injured tone in her voice. "I wanted to tell you, Eunice, but I couldn't. You have such a low opinion of men that I figured you'd flip out when I told you about Kane." She went on to tell her about how she'd written to him in prison the past year. "He wants to make a fresh start, that's all."

"And you believe in him?"

"Very much so."

Eunice seemed to ponder it. Mel wondered if she was about to get a lecture. She knew Eunice could recall each and every bad experience she'd ever had with the opposite sex, beginning in third grade. Mel had heard them all numerous times. Had she let it cloud her own judgment?

"I'm sorry you felt you had to keep it from me because of my bad attitude," Eunice said. "I run my mouth a lot without thinking. That's probably one of the reasons I have such rotten luck with men." She smiled gently. "I want you to be careful, honey. Sometimes that heart of yours is too soft for your own good. I'd hate to see it broken."

Mel nodded. Finally, she changed the subject, concentrating instead on business: what they had in inventory and what they expected to receive on the delivery truck that afternoon. There were two weddings on the books, but both were going to be small and wouldn't require anything out of the ordinary. If somebody needed something at the last minute, there were plenty of silk and dried flower arrangements from which to choose.

"If something comes up, I can always work in the

evenings," Mel told her assistant. "We're not having choir practice this month since so many church members are taking their vacations right now."

"I'm sure we'll be fine," Eunice assured her, pausing from time to time as though she hoped Mel would say something more about the man everybody was talking about.

Mel didn't. But as she drove toward Abercrombie Grocery, her friend's warning rang out loud.

Sometimes that heart of yours is too soft for your own good. I'd hate to see it broken.

Kane was hard at work on the cabinets behind the meat case when Mel returned. She changed into her work clothes and spent the morning cleaning the windows inside and out till they sparkled. Then she mopped the floor, getting down on her hands and knees with a scrub brush.

"Come tell me what you think," Kane said, motioning for her to join him behind the meat case.

"It looks wonderful," she told him, and meant it. He had put cabinet doors on the shelves to prevent them from looking cluttered. Not only that, he'd scrubbed the slicer and the meat case until they looked new. "All that's left is painting them. Dad and I can do that."

Kane looked pleased with her comments. "I can

help if you need me, but I've set up a few interviews for tomorrow."

They returned home tired and dirty. Once they took turns showering, Mel rummaged through the refrigerator for leftovers. There was still plenty of cold fried chicken from a couple of nights before.

"I hope this is okay," she said as they sat down at the table.

"This is great. I appreciate it."

They filled their plates and ate in silence for a moment. Mel was the first to speak. "I heard you and Dad up talking last night," she said. "What was that all about?" She had wanted to ask him all day but hadn't.

Kane glanced up from his plate and wondered how much of the conversation he should share. "He wanted to know how I felt about you."

Mel was clearly surprised by his words. "Wh-What did you tell him?"

Kane put his fork down. "The truth. I told him I thought I was falling in love with you."

She felt the room spin. "Why did you do that?"

"That's how I feel. What was I *supposed* to tell him?"

Mel put her own fork down and covered her face with her hands. She wasn't ready for this. All her insecurities sprang to life. "What did he say?"

"Actually, he took it very well."

Doubt gnawed at her. "I specifically asked you not to say anything about us or the way we feel," she said.

"Why are you so afraid for people to know?"

"I told you, it's personal." She started to take a bite; instead, she put her fork down and shoved her chair from the table.

"Where are you going?"

"I'm not hungry." She picked up her plate and carried it to the sink.

Kane stood as well and approached her. "Look, I'm sorry if I spoke out of turn, but I happen to like your father. I didn't want to lie." She kept her back to him. He could feel his anger stirring. "And you wouldn't feel the need to hide your own feelings if you weren't ashamed of me."

Mel whirled around and faced him. "I'm not ashamed of you. But I refuse to let you make a fool of me."

Now he was confused. "How will I do that?"

"Kane, you aren't going to want to hang around this town forever. One day you'll get a wild hair, and you'll be gone."

"Just like your mother, right?" The color drained from her face. "Isn't that what this is all about?" he demanded. "You're scared I'm going to leave you the way she did."

"One has nothing to do with the other."

"I think it does. I think that's the only reason you go out with Harper Beckwood. He's not likely to run off."

"You think you've got me all figured out, don't you?"

"Not at all. The only thing I know is that I'm crazy about you." He pulled her into his arms. "And I think you feel the same way about me."

She collapsed against him. Tears stung her eyes. "Why are you saying these things to me?" she cried.

"Because I mean it, baby." He put his hands on either side of her face and raised it so that she was looking directly into his eyes. "I cared for you long before I ever met you. You showed me the good things in life . . . things I hadn't seen much of. You'll never know what your letters meant to me, Mel."

His own eyes teared, and he shook his head sadly. "There are things you don't know about me, Mel. I can't make you understand how bad it was back there. I watched a man beaten to a pulp for snitching on someone. I saw another man raped in the basement while a gang of the worst scum you can imagine held him down."

"Oh, Kane." She put her arms around him. She felt like sobbing. "How do you ever get over something like prison?"

He kissed her forehead. "You take one day at a time, babe. You try to find something good around

you. It's easier for me to deal with because of you."
He kissed her softly.

Mel felt her heart burst with emotion. "Kane?"

"Hmmm?"

"I wish—" She paused and swallowed. "I wish we could make love."

At first he thought he'd misunderstood. He gazed at her, searching her face for some sign of uncertainty. He saw none. "Is that what you want?" He held his breath for her answer. She nodded, and he was suddenly thankful he'd visited the men's bathroom at the Wayside Tavern. He'd been seventeen years old the last time he'd purchased a condom in such a place.

"We can, baby," he said at last. "We can."

TWELVE

The bedroom was dim except for the light that spilled out from the closet, casting a soft glow on the embracing couple and leaving everything else swathed in shadows.

"Are you okay?" Kane asked, speaking against her parted lips. The last thing he wanted to do was make her nervous. He was nervous enough for both of them.

Mel gazed into his black eyes. "I'm fine." Under other circumstances she would have been a wreck, but the deep caring she saw on Kane's face convinced her she was doing the right thing.

"You should know something," he said. "I know we're using protection and all, but I'm clean. I've had all the tests, and I *do* mean all of them."

Mel smiled tenderly, loving him for caring enough to reassure her.

He kissed her again, this time hungrily. Mel felt herself being lowered onto the bed, felt the mattress dip beneath his weight as Kane joined her and gathered her up in his arms. She responded, parting her lips when he prodded them open with his tongue. Her head went into a slow spin.

Soon mere kisses weren't enough. Mel shifted on the bed restlessly, feeling the tension build low in her belly. When Kane reached for the buttons on her blouse, she was only too happy to help him. She shrugged off the garment and tossed it aside like an afterthought. Kane unfastened her bra, then slid the straps off her shoulders.

"You're beautiful," he said, gazing at her lush breasts in the dim light and wondering why Mel felt she had to hide from him by keeping the lights low. He hoped there'd come a day when she would let him make love to her in broad daylight. Still, he was more than content with what he had. Had a woman ever been this soft? Or smelled so sweet?

Suddenly, he was filled with a sense of foreboding. Fleeting pictures of prison life entered his mind, stealing from him the pleasure of holding Mel in his arms. He stiffened.

"Is something wrong?" Mel asked, sensing his mood change immediately.

Kane snapped back to the present and saw the uncertainty on her face. He shoved the unwelcome thoughts aside. He wasn't going to be haunted by demon memories tonight. "Everything's perfect," he said. He lowered his head.

Mel took a deep, shuddering breath as Kane's tongue swirled around the nipple, warm and moist, dredging up sensations deep inside. She covered his head with her hands, loving the feel of his coarse black hair against her fingers, his roughened jaw against her flesh. Below, their legs tangled like loving vines.

Kane pressed his body against her, and Mel felt his hardness. Even in her uncertainty, her own desire flared.

Suddenly, their clothes got in the way. Mel was as eager to be free of hers as Kane was. While he worked at the fastening of her shorts with frantic fingers, she undid the buttons on his shirt. They didn't pause until they were both naked beside each other.

"Oh, Mel." Kane's sigh was as soft as a summer breeze.

Mel gazed back at him through eyes that were unsure. She had never seen anything as magnificent as Kane Stoddard in the nude, lean and brown and perfectly proportioned. His chest was matted with springy black hair. It grew sparse over his stomach, then bushed at the apex of his thighs. She sucked her breath in sharply at the sight of his hardness.

As if reading her thoughts, Kane took one of her hands in his. "It's okay, Mel," he whispered. "Touch me." He brought her hand closer.

Mel touched him with tentative fingers. As hard as he was, it was impossible to believe it was only a muscle. She ran her fingers the length of it, wishing for once there was enough light to see the swollen shaft. Her fingers trembled as she touched the velvety tip. It was moist.

Kane closed his hand around hers and pulled it away. "I'm afraid I'm already too excited," he said.

"Because it has been so long for you?" she asked, knowing three years was a long time for a man to be celibate.

His smile was wry. "No, because of you, Melanie Abercrombie. I've been having fantasies about you since I received your first letter."

Mel tried to decide if that was just a line or if he meant it. When he looked at her that way, it was easy to forget folks thought her the plainer of the Abercrombie sisters. She felt beautiful for the first time in her life. She felt desired. She kissed him back, lingeringly, savoring the taste of his mouth.

Then he stroked her legs apart, and all logical thought ceased.

Reclaiming her lips, Kane crushed her to him. He skimmed her thighs with his hands before searching out her femininity. He smiled when he found her hot and wet. He dipped his fingers inside and heard her moan. It was like music to his ears.

Mel felt him shift on the bed. Once more he kissed her breasts; he kissed their undersides where they fell like half-moons against her rib cage. He flicked her navel with his tongue until she squirmed. He moved across her flat belly.

Her eyes flew open the minute his mouth made contact with that part of her body. Her mouth formed an O, half surprise, half protest. She stiffened. "Kane?"

He raised up slightly. "It's okay, baby. Trust me."

She could not deny what his touch was doing to her. She tried to resist giving in to it, but she was lost. Passion roared in her ears. She felt ignited. His tongue found the very source of her desire and sent her to even higher levels of ecstasy. She grasped his head with her hands and held on, soaring higher and higher, until the pleasure was too much. She arched against him, cried out, felt the room spin around her.

Mel felt Kane pull away for a moment and knew he was taking the necessary precautions to keep her from getting pregnant.

Finally, he swept her thighs apart and moved over her. He probed gently. "Am I hurting you?"

She shook her head. "No."

At last he entered her, and the sensations were so wonderful, it was all Kane could do to be still and let her body absorb the shock of him. "Are you okay?" he rasped out.

Mel arched against him. "I've never been better."

Kane started moving against her, slowly, carefully,

not wanting to do anything to cause her pain, not wanting to lose control and spoil it for her. Mel, he discovered, was an eager participant. She arched and met each thrust with an abandon he had not expected in her inexperience.

Once again, desire coursed through her body. Mel cried out softly with the intensity of it. Kane followed closely behind, shuddering in her arms.

When Mel opened her eyes sometime later, she found herself cuddled up to Kane. As though sensing she was now awake, he opened his eyes. "I've been waiting for you to wake up," he said.

She suddenly felt shy with him. "How long did I sleep?"

"Couple of hours. I figured you needed it. I drifted off a couple of times myself."

She gazed back at him. There didn't seem to be anything to say.

Kane sensed her uncertainty. "Any regrets?"

She shook her head. "Do you have regrets, Kane?" she asked, scared that he might.

He gazed at the ceiling. "I haven't deflowered many virgins in my time. I wouldn't like to think I might have forced you into a decision you wouldn't have made under normal conditions."

"I wanted us to make love, Kane and I'm not sorry we did it."

Relieved, he hugged her to him. "I keep thinking Harper would have been a better choice."

"Harper? I thought you—"

"I know what I've said about Harper, but he's in a much better position to offer you marriage than I am."

"Is that what this is about? You think I expect you to marry me now that we've made love? Do you think I'll pressure you into something you're not ready for?" Mel raised up and searched for her clothes. She was hurt.

Kane reached for her, but she shrugged him off. "All I'm saying is, you deserve a good man to take care of you."

"Who says I need taking care of, Kane Stoddard?"

"You want a family, don't you? You want security and stability and all those things. I've never been *any* of those things."

Mel retrieved her underthings, blushing wildly when the sheet fell and exposed her breasts. "Why don't you let *me* be the judge of what I want?"

"Everything I've ever touched has turned rotten," he said.

"What is this?" Mel asked, wondering why he was tormenting himself so. "Why are you doing this to yourself?"

"Because," he said simply. "Because I've fallen in love with you, and I'm scared."

Mel sat there wondering if she'd heard him right.

He'd said he was in love with her. Her heart swelled with emotion. "Why are you scared, Kane? Because you think I'll try to talk you into having children when you're not ready?"

He shook his head. "I'm scared because you deserve nothing less than that, and I'm not able to give it to you right now." He sighed and stacked his hands beneath his head. "When I was in prison, I couldn't wait to get out and do the things I wanted. I had everything planned. I was going to come here and find a job—"

"It's only been a couple of weeks, for heaven's sake."

"When you've lost three years of your life, two weeks is a lot of time to waste." He looked at her. "That's not all of it, though. I want to get my life on track because I have so much I need to make up for. I really was a sorry cuss before I went to prison, Mel. Leavenworth was not my first time behind bars. Why do you think it was so easy for a jury to convict me? They took one look at me and knew I was a punk."

"That's in the past," she said matter-of-factly. "The Kane Stoddard I know is a caring, giving man. You've got a few things to work out, but hey, we all do."

He pondered her words. "Is that how you see me? Caring and giving?"

"Absolutely."

It warmed him inside. "When you say it like that, I almost believe it."

She touched his cheek with her hand. "Then I suppose I'll have to say it to you every day."

He closed his own hand around hers, brought it to his face, and kissed her open palm. "Would you believe I want to make love to you again?" he said softly.

She arched one brow. "So soon? What about—" Her face grew pink. "You know."

He grinned. "I bought an extra one just in case."

Kane squared his shoulders and walked through the front door of Goulds' Graphics and Printing. A frustrated Mrs. Gould stood at the counter with a high school girl, trying to explain how to write up a job order. In the next room he could hear the steady *clack-clack-clack* of the printing press. The woman frowned at him, and Kane knew she recognized him.

"Is Mr. Gould in?" he asked, thinking he stood a better chance with her husband.

"He's busy. May I help you?" The woman looked harried and impatient to be about her work.

"I was in the neighborhood and decided to check back and see if you're hiring," Kane said. He had two interviews in town, but neither of the jobs sounded promising. This one, he knew, could lead to something.

"We're not hiring, Mr. Stoddard. I believe we covered that last time you were here."

So she did remember him. "That's too bad, Mrs. Gould. From what I hear, you're up to your eyeballs in work. I also hear folks are taking their business to Pelzer 'cause you're so far behind." The woman's face grew red, and he figured he'd gone too far. "Shame of it is, I could help you out of your bind. There isn't anything I don't know about running a print shop."

"Yes, I believe you learned it all behind bars," she said coolly. "Which is why I can't believe Melanie Abercrombie has opened her doors to the likes of you."

Kane felt his face grow hot. He placed his hands palms down on the counter and leaned closer. "Look, Mrs. Gould, I've already paid for one crime I didn't commit. Now, as far as Miss Abercrombie is concerned—"

"She's a fair and decent human being," the woman said.

"Funny you should say that, Mrs. Gould, 'cause that's exactly what Mel said about you and your husband."

The woman pulled herself up to her full height. "What do you want from me, Mr. Stoddard?" she said at last.

He gave her a sincere smile. The poor high school girl looked as if she'd rather be someplace else. "Just the chance to prove myself. Nothing more, nothing less."

Mrs. Gould looked torn. She eyed the stack of work orders beside her. The phone rang, and she snatched it up and mumbled an apology for a job that had taken longer to complete than she'd estimated. She hung up the phone and all but glared at Kane. Finally, she sighed, and her massive chest heaved with the effort. "You realize you'd be on probation the first two weeks? I make no guarantees after that."

Kane knew he could impress the hell out of them in that length of time. He held out his hand. "You've got yourself a deal, Mrs. Gould."

The woman hesitated, then put her own hand in his. "Be here at eight o'clock sharp tomorrow." She turned away, letting him know their conversation had come to an end.

THIRTEEN

"Surprise!"

Kane stumbled to a halt inside the kitchen door as Mel and Wilton cried out their greeting and threw handfuls of colorful confetti in his face. He caught a glimpse of a large sheet cake on the table with the word "Congratulations" spelled out in red letters.

"What's this?" he said. "It's not my birthday."

"Mrs. Gould called me at the store and said she'd given you a job. Congratulations, Kane."

"Mrs. Gould called *you*?"

"Uh-huh. Seemed very happy to have you aboard, as a matter of fact." That wasn't exactly true, Mel realized. Ann Gould had wanted to find out all she could about Kane. Mel suspected she was having second thoughts about hiring him, but after she'd bragged about Kane for twenty minutes, the woman seemed satisfied with her decision.

Kane gazed back in disbelief. He'd taken a two-hour motorcycle ride to celebrate his victory, but he could still remember Mrs. Gould's reluctance to hire him. "Are you sure we're talking about the same woman here?"

Mel chuckled. "Don't let that perpetual frown fool you," she said. "Mrs. Gould is actually very nice once you get to know her. I told you she's in my Sunday school class."

Kane took a closer look at the cake. He raised his eyes to Mel's radiant face. "How did you have time to bake this?" he asked.

"She didn't bake it," Wilton said. "She raced to the Thrifty Sak and bought it ready-made."

"Well, I blew up the balloons," Mel said, pointing to a batch of red and white balloons tied to one of the blades on the ceiling fan.

"Who helped you?" her father asked.

Kane was still gazing at her warmly. "Thank you," he said. "I can't remember when anyone has ever done something so nice for me."

Mel realized it was the second time he'd said those same words. It made her wonder if he'd known any nice people growing up. "Well, you'll have to wait until after dinner to have a piece of the cake," she said. "Otherwise, it'll spoil your appetite."

"My appetite is just fine, Miz Abercrombie," he said, his tone making it obvious to Mel he wasn't talking about food. She'd opened her mouth to reply, when someone banged on the front door.

"Wonder who that is?" she said. The banging became louder.

Wilton and Kane hurried into the living room after her. It sounded as though someone wanted to tear the door down. Kane rushed forward. "Let me get it," he said. Mel beat him to it.

Harper Beckwood rushed through the door with the speed and commotion of a freight train. "Where is he?" he demanded of Mel. "Where is that sorry, no-count—"

"You looking for me, Beckwood?" Kane said, closing the distance between the man and himself.

Harper glared at him. "I should have known you'd get her in your bed," he said. "It's all over town how the two of you are doing it right under her daddy's roof."

"Harper!" Mel's face flamed a bright red.

"Now, wait a dern minute," Wilton said, his own temper rising.

Harper swung his gaze in Mel's direction. "What's gotten into you? You're nothing but a—"

Kane grabbed him by the shirt collar. "Don't say it, Beckwood," he warned, his tone deadly.

"What do you care? You're the one who turned her into a whore."

Kane was filled with a rage like he'd never known. Without hesitating, he punched Harper right in the nose. The man stumbled backward, falling against the coffee table. Kane went after him.

Mel screamed. "Stop, you'll break the furniture," she cried, trying to think of a way to prevent a fight.

Kane was prevented from moving when someone grabbed the back of his collar. Surprised, he glanced back and found himself looking into Wilton's face.

"You lookin' to go back to prison?" the older man demanded. "If you mess up that man, that's exactly where you're going."

Kane looked from Wilton to a shocked Mel, then finally to Harper, who hadn't had the good sense to take off his suit coat before a fight. His anger cooled. Finally, Kane dragged the other man to his feet. "Get the hell out of here, Beckwood," he said, his breathing ragged, "before I change my mind."

With his nose bleeding profusely, Harper staggered away, ignoring Mel's offer to put ice on it. Kane turned to her, opened his mouth to apologize, then hesitated when he saw the fear in her eyes. Without a word she rushed down the hall to her bedroom.

The tension at the dinner table was thick enough to chew. Kane glanced across the table at Mel and Wilton and saw they were as uncomfortable as he was. Mel picked at her food as if the thought of eating it was more than she could bear. Finally, she shoved her chair from the table.

"Would you excuse me?" she said. "I'm not very hungry."

Kane watched her walk away. He put down his fork and tossed Wilton an apologetic look. " 'Fraid

I'm not hungry either." He pushed away from the table and left the kitchen.

Kane knocked on Mel's door a moment later. She looked surprised to see him. "Can we talk for a minute?" he said.

She opened the door wide for him to pass through, then closed it and made her way to the ruffled bed where she grabbed a throw pillow and pretended to study the fine lace stitching. "I'm listening," she said.

"I'm sorry I got carried away with Harper," he told her. His dark earnest eyes sought hers.

She leveled her gaze at him. Her expression was tight with strain. "Carried away? Is that what you call it?"

"You heard what he called you. Did you expect me to just stand there and do nothing?"

"Maybe Harper's right."

"Mel, no!" Kane went to her, grabbed both shoulders, and shook her slightly. "Don't say that, babe. Don't even think it."

"I fell into bed with you quick enough, didn't I? What's it been, two weeks we've known each other?"

His eyes beseeched her. "I've known you a helluva lot longer than two weeks, Melanie Abercrombie."

"Letters don't count."

"Letters *do* count. And I know things you didn't tell me in those letters. I know you can't stand to wake up to a dirty kitchen and that you don't talk to anybody until you've had at least two cups of coffee. I know you love tomatoes and would eat them for every meal if they didn't make your face break out. I know you buy all the latest fragrances in bubble bath but seldom take time for anything more than a quick shower. I know—"

"You've made your point, Kane."

He raised up. "Good."

"But that still doesn't change how I feel. I need more time. I want to know if what we have is real."

He looked hurt. "I'm sorry if you're feeling guilty about us making love," he said. "You certainly hid it well. Looked to me you were enjoying it as much as I was." He didn't give her a chance to respond. He jerked open the bedroom door and made his way out.

Wilton was drinking coffee and reading his newspaper when Kane made his way into the kitchen the following morning. "Where's Mel?" he said, accustomed to finding her at the table in her bathrobe. He wanted her to be there to share his excitement of getting ready to go to his new job.

"She's having coffee in her room this morning," Wilton said. "I wouldn't bother her if I were you. Harper called while you were in the shower. He had to go to the emergency room for his nose. Said they took X rays and found it broken in three places."

Kane paused in pouring his coffee. "I only hit him once." Wilton merely shrugged. "Are you mad at me too?" Kane asked the man.

Wilton shook his head. "Naw. The way I figure, any man who calls my daughter what he did deserves a broken nose."

Kane arrived at Goulds' Graphics and Printing at precisely eight clock. He found Mrs. Gould at the typesetter, frowning and looking harried even at this early hour. "We're swamped, and I don't have time to train you right now," she said.

He wanted to tell her he didn't need training, then decided it would be better to show her instead.

"Just go in the back and see if you can help my husband," she told him.

Kane pushed through the heavy curtain that separated the front office from the work area. He wrinkled his nose when he smelled onions coming from somewhere. The room was spacious, surrounded by shelves of brightly colored paper. There was a drafting table of sorts where he assumed the arts and graphics were done, on top of which rested several styrofoam coffee cups and a dried-up doughnut. One of the cups had spilled onto the table and the coffee left to dry. Next to the automatic folding machine a cutting table was littered with bits and pieces of paper in an assortment of colors. He wondered when the floor around it had been swept last. A mountain of work orders sat on another table, where someone had left a half-eaten hamburger with onions.

Kane decided he was going to have to work late to get the place in order.

He found Mr. Gould sipping coffee and tinkering with one of the presses while the other one ran at full speed. The man was a head shorter than his wife and looked to weigh a good fifty pounds less. He smiled when he spotted Kane.

"You must be Mr. Stoddard," he said, offering his hand. "My name's Sam. You want a cup of coffee?" When Kane shook his head, the man went on. "You'll have to excuse the mess. I been so snowed under, I haven't had a chance to pick up. The missus would have a fit if she saw it. Which is why I don't allow her back here." He paused and took a sip of his coffee. "She and I have an understanding. I stay outta her business, and she stays outta mine. You ever been married, Mr. Stoddard?"

Kane liked Sam Gould immediately, and he realized the only other time he'd felt that way was when he'd met Wilton Abercrombie. "Call me Kane," he said. "And no, I've never been married."

"I thought you looked smart the minute I laid eyes on you."

Kane chuckled. "Well, it can't be easy with a husband and wife working together."

"There's a secret to it," Sam told him, then drained the rest of his coffee and set the empty cup on top of the printing press. "You've got to set rules in the beginning. This is my territory, and that is her territory." He pointed to the curtain. "And you can't let it bother you when she gets in a tizzy 'cause we're behind. Sometimes, she pokes her head through that curtain and yells at me for not having an order out on time, but I let it slide right down my back. Otherwise, I'd have ulcers like folks in the big cities do. See this water pistol?" he said, picking up a plastic gun. "She starts sticking her head through that curtain too often, and I wet her down good. Makes her mad 'cause she has her hair done every week and has to keep it that way till her next appointment. Wraps it in toilet paper every night so it won't get messed up."

Kane nodded, trying to keep a straight face. "How come you're only running one press this morning when you've got such a workload?" he asked.

"Aw, this'un is acting up," he said. "Leaking brown fluid and making a mess on everything I try to run. I called a repairman, but he can't make it out till sometime tomorrow. Reckon we'll have to work with one, though it'll put us further behind. I'll have to fill up the gun."

"You got any tools?" Kane asked. "So I can take

it apart and look at it?" He suspected neither press had been cleaned in a while.

"Sure I got tools. But I don't have an inkling what's wrong with it, and I never had much time to learn how to work on these things."

"Well, it's lucky for you that I know everything there is to know about them," Kane said, remembering how many times he'd watched the repairman take them apart in prison. He'd stayed and watched because it had kept him from going back to his cell. "Besides," he added, "I don't think there's much wrong with it that a good cleaning won't take care of."

"A good cleaning?" The way Sam said it, one would have thought Kane had taught him a string of new French words.

"Yeah, I don't know for sure, but I have a feeling that somebody might have spilled a cup of coffee on it, and it got down in the parts."

A look of alarm passed over Sam's face, telling Kane he knew he'd been caught red-handed. "Don't tell the missus."

Kane grinned. He was going to like working there. "I wouldn't think of it, Sam."

Mel was cool toward Kane for the rest of the week, speaking to him only when necessary. Kane had never felt so miserable in his life. He wanted to tell her how well his new job was going, how pleased the Goulds were with his work and the fact he'd been able to repair some of their equipment, but the look on her face didn't invite conversation, so he kept his mouth shut. He arrived home after work and helped her with the chores, then, once dinner was over, walked Rover and sat with Wilton in front of the television set. Wilton wasn't the same either. Kane wasn't sure what was going on with the man; he seemed preoccupied.

"Blair will be home next weekend," Wilton announced at dinner on Sunday. "I called her to find out how the commercial was going. They're supposed to wrap things up in a couple of days, then she plans to spend a few days on the beach." He paused. "She met a man. He's driving her back."

"That's nice," Mel said, trying to keep the surprise out of her voice. Blair certainly hadn't wasted any time finding someone. But then, she never did.

"There's something else," Wilton said, his tone causing Mel to look up from her meal. "Your mother is going to join us for dinner next Sunday."

Mel gazed back at her father with a look of outright bewilderment. How could Adelle be coming to dinner? She lived all the way in Louisiana. "You're joking, right?"

"I'm perfectly serious. That's why I put in a call to Blair. I want her here when your mother arrives."

Mel's mind refused to register the significance of his words. He *wasn't* kidding. He must've called Adelle after he'd read the letters. "Daddy, how could you?" she demanded, a faint thread of hysteria running through her voice.

Kane shifted uncomfortably in his chair. "Do y'all want me to leave?"

"No, stay," Wilton told him. He turned back to his daughter. "I invited Adelle because she has a right to see you girls after all these years."

It took a moment for his words to sink in. "She abandoned us; she has no rights."

"It was as much my fault as it was hers."

Anger raged through her. "How can you say that? You stayed and took care of us."

Wilton put down his napkin. His face was clouded with despair. "Your mother was unhappy, and I did nothing to change that for her."

"What were you *supposed* to do?"

Wilton almost sagged with regret. "I was at the store all the time. I never took her anywhere. She was stuck in this house morning, noon, and night. I took her for granted."

"I'm not going to let you take the blame for this, Daddy," she said, reaching across the table to cover his hand.

"You don't understand, honey. My marriage to Adelle was arranged by her father. She was only sixteen years old; I was almost twice her age. Her family was poor. It was a relief to them to have one less mouth to feed." He paused and seemed to reflect. "She wasn't happy, and I knew it. All I wanted was someone to take care of the house and the kids."

Mel swallowed the lump in her throat. It was unthinkable that her father should invite Adelle back after all these years. "You should have told me you were going to call her. I had a right to know. After all, I'm the one who had to take over when she left." Tears filled her eyes.

"It's not right to hold grudges, Melanie."

She shoved her chair away from the table and tossed her napkin on her plate.

"Where are you going?" Wilton asked.

"Out!" Without another word Mel let herself out the back door.

Wilton started to get up and go after her, but Kane stopped him. "I'll see about her."

Kane found her sitting on the swing in the backyard. She glanced up at him, and he could see the tears in her eyes. "Daddy put this swing up when I was eight years old," she told him. "Who would have thought it would last this long?"

He knew she didn't want to talk about an old childhood swing any more than he did. "Are you okay, Mel?" he asked softly.

"No, I'm not okay. I'm mad as hell, that's what I am. Daddy has no right to bring that . . . that woman into this house after what she did to us."

"That woman happens to be your mother," he reminded her.

Mel snapped her head up. "Don't try to defend her, Kane. You said it yourself—anybody can give birth to children. The hard part is raising them. As far as I'm concerned, Adelle Taylor . . . that's her name now . . . has no right to disrupt this family."

Kane saw that she was trying desperately to keep from crying. "Maybe she wants to apologize."

Mel glanced away. "I wouldn't accept her apology if she held a gun to my head." When he didn't say anything, she went on. "You don't know how it was, trying to take care of everybody."

He reached for her hand and held it. "I can imagine, Mel. You're still doing it."

She was quiet for a moment. "I despise the woman for what she did. It's as simple as that. There's no hope of a reconciliation."

"No hope?" he asked. He glanced at the Doberman straining the chain in order to get closer. Kane walked over to him and unhooked the chain from his collar. The dog leaped up and put his front paws on Kane's chest. He chuckled and stroked the animal affectionately.

"You once told me there's always hope," he said, bending down to pick up a stick. "Just look at Rover here." He tossed the stick, and the dog took off, then brought it back with his nubby tail wagging.

Mel smiled at the sight. In a short period of time, Kane had won the dog's trust, and they'd become best buddies.

She gazed at him, taking in the handsome face, the powerful shoulders. She had missed talking to him, missed spending time with him, kissing him. She'd wanted to ask about his new job all week, but she was still hurt over how he'd reacted to Harper. As much as she appreciated him defending her, he had to learn he could not go through life using his fists every time he didn't like something. She'd called Harper personally to apologize, but the man didn't have much to say to her. She'd ended up talking with Amy instead, and they'd made plans to go out for ice cream the following week. She wasn't about to let Harper stand in the way of their friendship.

Mel watched Kane toss the stick once more. This time Rover took off in the opposite direction. She laughed out loud. Their gazes met and locked.

"You still furious with me?" Kane asked.

"No."

"Good." He pulled her up from the swing so that she was facing him. "I've missed you, Mel. They threw me in solitary for two weeks once, and I don't think it was half as bad as having you mad at me."

"Why were you put in solitary?"

Kane suddenly wished he hadn't brought it up. "I refused to snitch on someone." He shrugged. "It wasn't a big deal." He slid his arms around her waist. "I try not to think about things like that. I'm sorry I brought it up."

Mel studied him for a moment in silence. "You can't block out three years of your life, Kane. There must've been something positive out of the whole thing."

He thought about it. "I guess so. I would never have met Dave Resnick, the prison psychologist, who told me I had a chip on my shoulder. He believed I was innocent when nobody else did. Anyway, he's the one who convinced me to start working toward a college education. Otherwise, I would have wasted those years."

"I'm glad he was there for you," Mel said gently.

Kane squeezed her hand. "He wasn't the only one. You were there for me. You kept me going when I didn't think I would be able to take another day."

"I'm glad I could help."

Kane gazed at her for a moment and wondered how she could ever think herself plain. "You know, I've fallen in love with you. I think about you all day, and then I lie awake at night and think about you. You're everything I always wanted in my sorry life."

She was overjoyed at his announcement. She knew her own feelings were dangerously close to love. She wanted to make love to the man again and lie in his arms afterward. But she was afraid. What if he decided life in Hardeeville wasn't what he wanted?

What if his job at the printing company didn't work out? What if she fell head over heels in love with him, and he left? She would never get over it. "I care for you, too, Kane," she said at last. "But like I told you the other night, I need more time. To be sure."

He forced himself to smile. "Please don't make me wait too long, babe."

FOURTEEN

The following week dragged, during which time Mel said very little to her father. She could not remember a time when she'd been so angry at him. She was thankful they'd finished remodeling the store so she could return to the flower shop and Eunice's questioning looks.

She and Kane met for lunch every day, eating sandwiches on the rustic benches that lined the sidewalks on the courthouse lawn. They fed their leftovers to the squirrels. After three days people stopped staring when they walked by, and Eunice gave up trying to pry information out of her. It was obvious Melanie Abercrombie and her beau, Kane Stoddard, weren't going to talk about their relationship until they were darn good and ready.

In the evenings they took long walks, with Rover straining on a leash in front of them. Mel knew she wouldn't be able to get rid of the dog even if someone showed an interest. Kane, who claimed he'd never had a pet growing up, was much too attached, and he turned into an oversized kid when Rover was around.

On Tuesday they saw a Mel Gibson movie in town and shared a large buttered popcorn.

On Wednesday, with the chores behind them, they lay on Wilton's massive hammock and gazed at the stars.

They rented videos on Friday, old Clint Eastwood westerns, and stayed up half the night watching them and eating caramel corn.

They bought groceries on Saturday, and Kane insisted on paying for half now that he was a working man.

Mel realized she was growing to love him more each day.

She awoke in the wee hours of Sunday morning, slipping out of Blair's bedroom quietly so as not to wake her. The girl had arrived the night before with the new man in her life, a struggling actor who'd been chosen to play opposite her in the NuWave Wine Cooler commercial. From the way it sounded, both their careers had taken a turn in the right direction. Blair was even talking about taking him back to New York with her. Mel was glad when he didn't stay. She had enough on her mind without having to entertain another guest.

Mel turned on the kitchen light and went straight for the coffeemaker which she'd set up before going to bed. She flipped on the switch and listened as it gurgled to life. She waited for it to drip through as she thought about the day that lay ahead.

Adelle Taylor had also arrived in town the night before. Wilton had driven to the airport in Pelzer to pick her up, then drove her to the Restful Lodge in Hardeeville. Mel had been terrified her father would insist Adelle stay at the house, but luckily he hadn't. Perhaps he knew it would be pushing things.

Mel poured a cup of coffee and sat at the kitchen table. The reunion with her mother hovered over her like a storm cloud. Why had her father insisted on bringing the woman back in their home after all these years? Had he lost his mind? It was like a knife in the back to Mel, who'd taken care of everything all these years. Didn't anybody appreciate what she'd done?

Mel experienced a moment of guilt. Perhaps the reason her father had never remarried was because she had always taken care of him so well. Or maybe he hadn't married because he would have felt uncomfortable bringing a wife into the house he shared with his daughter. She pushed the thought aside as soon as it surfaced. She didn't want to believe it. She'd always thought she was doing her father a favor by staying.

"A penny for your thoughts," a masculine voice said.

Mel snapped her head up and found Kane standing at the opposite end of the table. "I didn't hear you get up," she said, feeling flustered. He wore a pair of jogging shorts and nothing else.

"What are you doing awake?" he asked. "It's not even five o'clock."

"I couldn't sleep. You want a cup of coffee?" The way she said it suggested she needed companionship more than coffee.

Kane noted the dark circles under her eyes and knew the reason for them. Instead of saying anything, he walked around to the back of her chair and raised his hands on her shoulders, where he began kneading the muscles. "You're tense," he said, leaning forward and brushing his lips along her nape. "I know just the thing to loosen you up."

Mel knew exactly what he had on his mind. Up till now he had heeded her warning that she needed more time, and he'd backed off. Perhaps he'd grown tired of waiting when it was obvious their relationship was growing stronger every day. "Someone might hear," she said.

He whispered in her ear. "There's always the attic. We could put one of those quilts on the floor."

Mel felt dizzy at the thought of slipping upstairs to the attic with him. She realized they wouldn't be discovered. Her father didn't get up until eight or nine o'clock on Sunday, and Blair wouldn't tumble out of bed till noon.

"Okay." She stood and reached for his hand. She held her fingers to her lips and they took to the stairs, trying carefully not to make any noise. Nevertheless, the wood creaked and groaned beneath their weight.

Mel didn't draw a breath of relief until they reached the small room upstairs. She turned to Kane. Suddenly, she felt very shy. She refused to make eye contact with him as she searched through a large box. She found two old quilts that smelled of mothballs and laid them on the floor. Kane reached for her.

Wordlessly, he eased her down on the blankets, then pulled her close, cushioning her head in the crook of his arm. Mel pressed against him, loving the feel of his solid warm body. She had missed this. Even as close as they'd been all week, she knew this physical aspect was just as important in a relationship.

His mouth was soft and warm on hers, prodding her lips apart with his tongue so he could explore. The kiss was slow and thorough, turning her thoughts to mush and awakening a need deep in her belly. Mel pressed her lower body against his and knew his need was as great as hers.

Kane broke the kiss, and they both gasped for air. "I want you, Mel," he said.

"I want you too."

Kane rained kisses over her face, against her

fluttering eyelids, and down her neck. He moved one hand down the length of her, the flare of her hip, her sloping thighs, then slipped it beneath her gown. Her flesh was warm and smooth. He pulled the gown upward. Mel raised up so he could get it over her head. He tossed it aside. Her panties joined the gown a moment later.

"Look how pretty you are," he whispered. Before she had a chance to respond, he bent over and took one rose-tipped nipple in his mouth. While he kissed both breasts, his hands explored the rest of her body, pausing between her thighs.

Mel reached for his shorts, suddenly impatient to have him naked beside her. Kane lifted his hips off the floor long enough so she could pull them down.

Their foreplay was made brief by their need. Kane entered her, easing his body slowly into her tightness so as not to hurt her. She felt no pain, only the exquisite pleasure of being filled by the man she loved.

They moved together slowly, savoring each sensation brought on by their coupling. Mel opened herself to him, inviting him deeper as her emotions whirled and her passion skidded out of control. The pleasure was both pure and explosive, and she bit her bottom lip to keep from crying out. Kane plunged, the look on his face somewhere between despair and ecstasy. He shuddered in her arms as he captured her mouth once more, sealing their union with a kiss.

It was several minutes before either moved. Kane slid off her body and gathered her into his arms as they waited for their breathing to return to normal.

"You know what we forgot." It wasn't a question but a statement.

Mel gasped as realization hit her. "Oh no." She raised up and reached for her gown. "How could I have been so stupid?"

"Hey, wait a minute," Kane said, pulling her back down. "It's as much my fault as yours."

"But what'll we do if—"

"If you end up pregnant?" he asked. When she nodded, he smiled gently. "Would that be so bad, Mel?"

"Of course it would be bad. We're not—" She didn't finish.

He pulled her close. "Why don't we worry about that when the time comes," he said. "Like your dad always says, there's no sense borrowing trouble."

Once again, she raised up. This time Kane didn't stop her. "We'd better get downstairs," she said. "I have a lot to do before church."

Kane reached for his shorts. There were so many things he wanted to tell her, that he loved her and would gladly marry her. But, financially, he wasn't able to. How could he afford a wife with what he made at the printing company? Of course, he would probably get salary raises as time went on, but that would take a while.

He had to think.

Adelle Taylor was an older, shrunken version of the woman Mel remembered. As Wilton led the frail woman through the front door and invited her to sit, Mel tried not to look shocked. What had happened to the lovely, vivacious woman who'd taught her girls to dance in this very living room? She looked haggard. Her hair, once a deep auburn color, was brittle and streaked with gray.

Mel suddenly wished Kane had not made some excuse about seeing to the dogs, because she truly needed his support right now. She wondered if he would always disappear the minute things got tough, and she realized she was still hurt over his lack of commitment that morning.

"Mama!" Blair literally threw herself against Adelle. "Mama, I'm so glad you're here."

Adelle's eyes teared as she hugged her youngest to her breast. "I knew you'd turn out to be a beauty," she said. Her eyes met Mel's and locked. "Hello, Melanie. You've turned into quite a beauty as well."

"Hello," Mel said, her voice as stiff as the Peter Pan collar on her dress. It annoyed her that Adelle felt she had to flatter her to win her over when there was no chance of that happening. "Would you like something cold to drink?" she asked.

"A glass of water would be nice."

Mel went into the kitchen for the water, just as Kane stepped through the back door, wearing the same outfit he'd worn to church, the same he'd worn to work each day. He paused at the look on her face. "Are you okay?"

"Please don't leave," she said, feeling very close to tears. "This is harder than I thought."

He put his arm around her. "I'm sorry, baby. I just didn't want to get in the way." He kissed her softly.

When Mel returned to the living room with the ice water, Kane was by her side. She introduced him to Adelle but didn't try to explain why he was there. Instead, she set the water down beside the woman and excused herself so she could finish dinner. Kane followed and set the table while she whipped the potatoes and poured the food into serving dishes.

Blair talked nonstop during the meal, telling Adelle all about the commercial she'd shot in Biloxi and the man she'd met and the fact that they'd been selected as the NuWave Wine Cooler couple. "But enough about me," Blair said. "Tell us what you've been doing all these years in Louisiana."

Adelle looked uncomfortable suddenly being thrust into the limelight. She scanned the group anxiously. "Well, there's not much to tell. I was married to a man who made his living in furniture. He died last year."

"Did you have any other children?" Blair asked, looking excited at the prospect of a half brother or sister.

"No, there weren't any children."

Mel was tempted to tell Adelle she was smart not to have more children since she couldn't handle the two she had. Instead, she bit back the retort and tried to concentrate on her meal. But she could have been eating cardboard for all she cared.

With dinner behind them, Wilton escorted Adelle into the living room, then excused himself and disappeared into the attic. Mel had a sinking feeling she knew what he'd gone after. Sure enough, he returned with the stack of photo albums. "Everybody gather round," he said. "We haven't looked at these in years." When Mel refused to budge from the doorway, he motioned for her to join him.

"No, Daddy," she said, fearing he'd lost his mind. "I don't care to travel down memory lane today. You'll have to go without me." She turned and made her way out of the room, but not before she saw the hurt look in his eyes.

"Where are you going?" Kane asked, as she headed for the back door.

"To clean the dog pen."

"I already have."

"I'll mow the lawn."

"I did that two days ago."

She turned and glared at him, her frustration growing with each breath she drew. "Then I'll clean the garage."

"In your church dress?"

"Yes!"

The look on her face didn't invite further comment. "Okay, I'll help you."

"I don't want your help," she sputtered.

Kane followed her out the door.

She stalked across the yard to the garage.

Kane reached for her hand and pulled her to a halt.

Mel whirled around and faced him. "I've spent eighteen years taking care of this family because that woman inside didn't want to do it. When Blair fell off her bicycle, *I* put the Band-Aid on her knee. *I'm* the one who told her how babies were really made, and when it was time, *I* helped her pick out her first bra. I've cooked and cleaned and ironed for my father, but not once has he ever said thank you."

"Why do you do it, Mel?" he asked softly.

Her eyes teared. "Because I thought they needed me. All this time—" A sob escaped her lips. "I should have started my own life."

Kane reached for her. "Oh, baby, don't cry."

"Don't touch me," she said. "You need a friend right now while you're starting out. As soon as you get on your feet and meet a few people, you'll be gone."

Sudden anger lit his eyes. "I'm tired of you comparing me to your mother. You're not the only one in this world who's been hurt or disappointed."

He walked away before she could respond.

FIFTEEN

It was late afternoon when Mel loaded the tall trash bags to the back of Wilton's truck and closed the door to the garage. "Well, if anybody's handing out blue ribbons for clean garages, I should win," she muttered to herself as she trudged up the steps to the house. She looked as if she'd spent the afternoon in a coal bin. Her dress was filthy and torn, her eyes swollen from having spent the past three hours crying.

Kane rode away shortly after their argument and hadn't returned. No doubt he was looking for a place to live. She didn't blame him. He was probably tired of hearing her bemoan the past. Nevertheless, she ached with the loss.

Mel opened the back door and stepped into the kitchen. She felt tired and drained. At the same time she wasn't angry anymore. If her father wanted to invite Adelle Taylor back into their lives, who was she to stop him? If Kane Stoddard decided to leave and she ended up pregnant and alone, well, she would have to deal with that as well. Folks would talk, naturally. She would no longer be poor plain Melanie Abercrombie who couldn't catch a man; she would be poor Melanie Abercrombie who went and got herself knocked up by the first man who looked twice at her. But she would get through it the way she had all the other difficult times in her life. As much as she loved and wanted Kane, she could not live in constant fear of him leaving.

Mel came to an abrupt halt when she spied her father sitting in the living room staring at a blank TV screen. He took one look at her appearance. "You look like something the cat would think twice about dragging in," he said. Mel shrugged and started to make her way down the hall, but he called her back. "Sit down, I want to talk to you."

"Shouldn't I clean up first?"

"This is more important." He indicated the chair next to him.

Mel took a seat. She thought he looked tired. Weary. "If it's about the way I behaved earlier, I'm sorry," she said. "I guess my feelings were hurt."

"Because I invited your mother to a simple dinner?"

Once again, Mel felt as though she'd cry. Why did she have to deal with this on top of losing Kane? "Daddy, you don't understand how hard it was for me when she left. I was a kid at the time, but I had to grow up overnight. And now, almost twenty years later, you invite her into this house as though none of it ever happened."

"I shouldn't have let you take on all that responsibility," he said mournfully. "I should have hired someone to come in."

"I knew we didn't have the money for that."

"I should have asked your grandmother for help. But I was too proud. I didn't want anyone to know how your mother had hurt me. I ended up taking you for granted the way I'd done your mother. You should have been going out on dates; instead, you sat home with me. You should have been married a long time ago, but you've stayed here because I was too lazy and set in my ways to learn how to"—he paused, then choked out the last words—"take care of myself."

Mel flew to his side, her heart turning over in her chest at the sight of his tears. "Oh, Daddy, don't cry," she pleaded. "Please don't cry. I did it because I wanted to. Don't you see, nobody forced me."

Wilton covered his daughter's head with his hands. "I never even thanked you for all you've done," he managed, his voice shaking.

Mel looked up, her own eyes tearful. "You don't have to thank me. We're family. We're supposed to look after each other. No matter what."

He pulled her close. "Then maybe you can understand why I have to help your mother," he said. "Why

I have to forgive her the past and be here for her now." He paused and sighed heavily, and the sound seemed to come from deep inside. "Your mother is dying, Mel. No matter what happened in the past, we have to be here for her now."

It was late when Mel heard Kane pull up on his motorcycle. Heart thudding in her chest, she slipped out of her bedroom in her gown and tiptoed down the hall toward the kitchen. She let herself out the back door just as he was starting up the steps. They both paused when they saw each other.

Mel clasped her hands together tightly. Just the sight of him caused her pulse to beat erratically. Had he come for his clothes? Had she realized how much she loved him only to lose him now? "I wanted to apologize," she told him, her voice thick and unsteady. When he didn't answer, she went on, almost shyly. "I figured you were gone for good."

Kane took a step toward her, thinking she had never looked more beautiful than she did at that moment with her hair hanging down and the moon shining on her face. He had spent the afternoon on a riverbank, coming to terms with his past and pondering his future. He'd let go of some of his anger. It was time to let the wounds heal, he'd decided, although the prison psychologist had been telling him that for years. Nevertheless, he was filled with a strange sense of peace.

"I wouldn't do that to you, Mel," he said at last. "Not without saying good-bye. And not unless you wanted me to go."

She fidgeted with her hands. "I don't want you to go, Kane. Ever."

He was almost weak with relief. He closed the distance between them and took one of her hands in his. "Do you mean that?"

She nodded. "And not because there's a chance I could have gotten pregnant. I love you."

He didn't think it was possible to feel so good over three simple words. "I love you, too, Mel. I have for a long time now. When I told you how much you helped me while I was in prison, I meant it. Without you I would never have found the strength to go on." He raised her hand to his lips and kissed it. "And I wouldn't mind at all if you got pregnant."

Her heart leaped for joy. "Really?"

He took a seat on one step and pulled her onto his lap. "Listen, Mel, I've been doing a lot of thinking this afternoon. I don't have much to offer you right now—"

"I don't need anything," she said.

He smiled. "A man still likes to think he can provide for the woman he loves. In short, I've decided to go back to school and get that degree in architecture."

"That's wonderful!"

"Yes, but I'll have to attend at night so I can work at the print shop during the day. It'll only be for a year or so. I promise I'll try to get my degree as quickly as possible, but it might be tough for a while."

"We'll have the weekends, won't we?" she asked.

"Yes, we'll have the weekends. And the nights."

"And I can help you study, right?"

He grinned. "I'm counting on it."

She hesitated. "You'll continue to live here with Dad and me?"

He chuckled. "Well, I hope so." At the blank look she shot him, he went on. "Mel, darling, do you not realize this is a marriage proposal?"

She shrieked and almost fell off his lap. Kane grabbed her in the nick of time. "You're asking me to marry you?" she shouted in glee. "I'm sorry, I didn't catch that. But then, I haven't had much experience in the marriage-proposal department."

"You have now," he said, "although I honestly wasn't expecting this much enthusiasm. Does this mean you'll marry me?"

Mel threw her arms around his neck and hugged him for all she was worth. Suddenly, she pulled back. "You're not doing this because you think I might be . . . you know?"

He shook his head, and his look was sincere. "No, darling. I'll take you with or without a baby."

"Oh, Kane!" She hugged him again. "We have to tell Daddy, although he might think a month is a bit quick."

"We can have a one- to two-month engagement if it'll make him feel better," he said. "Unless you're pregnant, of course, and want to do it quicker. I'm open." He paused. "Does this mean you aren't mad at your father anymore?"

Mel sobered instantly at the mention of her father. "We had a long talk. About my mother," she added, then paused. "Kane, she's dying. That's why she started writing after all these years. I never should have hidden those letters." She swallowed hard. She'd spent the entire evening trying to come to terms with all her father had told her. "Anyway, she wants to get to know her family once more before she goes."

"And you're okay with that?"

"I am now. From what Daddy told me tonight, she hasn't had a happy life. The only problem—" She let the sentence drop.

"What?"

Mel's eyes misted. She had cried more today than she had cried in her entire life. "I'm afraid of getting close to her. It's going to be tough having to say good-bye to her again."

He tightened his arms around her. "I'll help you through it, babe. I swear, you won't have to go through it alone. You'll never have to go through anything alone again."

Mel buried her face against his wide chest. She gave a contented sigh. It was nice to know he was planning to be around that long.

THE EDITOR'S CORNER

Summer is here at last, and we invite you to join us for our 11th anniversary. Things are really heating up with six wonderful new Loveswepts that sizzle with sexy heroes and dazzling heroines. As always, our romances are packed with tender emotion and steamy passion that are guaranteed to make this summer a hot one!

Always a favorite, Helen Mittermeyer gives us a heroine who is **MAGIC IN PASTEL**, Loveswept #690. When fashion model Pastel Marx gazes at Will Nordstrom, it's as if an earthquake hits him! Will desires her with an intensity that shocks him, but the anguish she tries to hide makes him want to protect her. Determined to help Pastel fight the demons that plague her, Will tries to comfort her, longing to know why his fairy-tale princess is imprisoned by her fear. Enveloped in the arms of a man whose touch soothes and arouses, Pastel struggles to accept the gift of his caring and keep their rare love true in a world of fire and ice. Helen delivers a story with characters that will warm your heart.

The heroine in Deborah Harmse's newest book finds herself **IN THE ARMS OF THE LAW,** Loveswept #691. Rebekah de Bieren decides Detective Mackenzie Hoyle has a handsome face, a great body, and a rotten attitude! When Mack asks Becky to help him persuade one of her students to testify in a murder case, he is stunned by this pint-sized blond angel who is as tempting as she is tough . . . but he refuses to take no for an answer—no matter how her blue eyes flash. Becky hears the sorrow behind Mack's cynical request and senses the tormented emotions he hides beneath his fierce dedication. Drawn to the fire she sees sparking in his cool gray eyes, she responds with shameless abandon—and makes him yearn for impossible dreams. Deborah Harmse will have you laughing and crying with this sexy romance.

FOR MEN ONLY, Loveswept #692, by the wonderfully talented Sally Goldenbaum, is a romance that cooks. The first time Ellie Livingston and Pete Webster met, he'd been a blind date from hell, but now he looks good enough to eat! Pete definitely has his doubts about taking a cooking class she's designed just for men, but his gaze is hungry for the pleasures only she can provide. Pete has learned not to trust beautiful women, but Ellie's smile is real—and full of temptation. Charmed by her spicy personality and passionate honesty, he revels in the sensual magic she weaves, but can Pete make her believe their love is enough? **FOR MEN ONLY** is a story you can really sink your teeth into.

Glenna McReynolds has given us another dark and dangerous hero in **THE DRAGON AND THE DOVE,** Loveswept #693. Cooper Daniels had asked for a female shark with an instinct for the jugular, but instead he's sent an angelfish in silk who looks too innocent to help him with his desperate quest to avenge his brother's death! Jessica Langston is fascinated by the hard sensuality of his face and mesmerized by eyes that meet hers with the force of a head-on collision, but she refuses to be dismissed—winning Cooper's respect and igniting his desire. Suddenly, Cooper is compelled by an inexorable need to claim her with tantalizing gentleness. Her surrender makes him yearn to rediscover the tenderness he's missed, but Cooper believes he'll only hurt the woman who has given him back his life. Jessica cherishes her tough hero, but now she must help heal the wounds that haunt his soul. **THE DRAGON AND THE DOVE** is Glenna at her heart-stopping best.

Donna Kauffman invites you to **TANGO IN PARADISE,** Loveswept #694. Jack Tango is devastatingly virile, outrageously seductive, and a definite danger to her peace of mind, but resort owner April Morgan needs his help enough to promise him whatever he wants—and she suspects what he wants is her in his arms! Jack wants her desperately but without regrets—and he'll wait until she pleads for his touch. April responds with wanton satisfaction to Jack's need to claim her soul, to possess and pleasure her, but even with him as her formidable ally, does she dare face old ghosts? **TANGO IN PARADISE** will show you why Donna is one of our brightest and fastest-rising stars.

Last, but definitely not least, is a battle of passion and will in Linda Wisdom's **O'HARA vs. WILDER,** Loveswept #695. For five years, Jake Wilder had been the man of her sexiest dreams, the best friend and partner she'd once dared to love, then leave, but seeing him again in the flesh leaves Tess O'Hara breathless . . . and wildly aroused! Capturing her mouth in a kiss that sears her to the toes and catches him in the fire-storm, Jake knows she is still more woman than any man can handle, but he is willing to try. Powerless to resist the kisses that brand her his forever, Tess fights the painful memories that their reckless past left her, but Jake insists they are a perfect team, in bed and out. Seduced by the electricity sizzling between them, tantalized beyond reason by Jake's wicked grin and rough edges, Tess wonders if a man who's always looked for trouble can settle for all she can give him. Linda Wisdom has another winner with **O'HARA vs. WILDER.**

Happy reading,

With warmest wishes,

Nita Taublib

Nita Taublib

Associate Publisher

P.S. Don't miss the women's novels coming your way in June—**WHERE SHADOWS GO,** by Eugenia Price, is an enthralling love story of the Old South that is the second volume of the *Georgia Trilogy*, following **BRIGHT CAPTIVITY; DARK JOURNEY,** by award-winning Sandra Canfield, is a heart-wrenching story of love and obsession, betrayal and forgiveness, in which a woman discovers the true price of forbidden passion; **SOME-THING BORROWED, SOMETHING BLUE,** by Jillian Karr, is a mixture of romance and suspense in which four brides—each with a dangerous secret—will be the focus of a deliciously glamorous issue of *Perfect Bride* magazine; and finally **THE MOON RIDER,** Virginia Lynn's most appealing historical romance to date, is a passionate tale of a highwayman and his lady-love. We'll be giving you a sneak peek at these wonderful books in next month's LOVESWEPTs. And immediately following this page look for a preview of the terrific romances from Bantam that are *available now*!

Don't miss these fantastic books by your favorite Bantam authors

On sale in April:

DECEPTION
by *Amanda Quick*

RELENTLESS
by *Patricia Potter*

SEIZED BY LOVE
by *Susan Johnson*

WILD CHILD
by *Suzanne Forster*

THE NEW YORK TIMES
BESTSELLING NOVEL

DECEPTION
by Amanda Quick

"One of the hottest and most prolific writers in romance today . . . Her heroines are always spunky women you'd love to know and her heroes are dashing guys you'd love to love."
—USA Today

NOW AVAILABLE IN PAPERBACK
WHEREVER BANTAM BOOKS ARE SOLD

Patricia Potter

Nationally Bestselling Author
Of **Notorious** and **Renegade**

RELENTLESS

*Beneath the outlaw's smoldering gaze, Shea Randall felt
a stab of pure panic . . . and a shiver of shocking desire.
Held against her will by the darkly handsome bandit,
she knew that for her father's sake she must find a
way to escape. Only later, as the days of her captivity
turned into weeks and Rafe Tyler's fiery passion sparked
her own, did Shea fully realize her perilous position—
locked in a mountain lair with a man who could steal
her heart . . .*

The door opened, and the bright light of the
afternoon sun almost blinded her. Her eyes were
drawn to the large figure in the doorway. Silhou-
etted by the sun behind him, Tyler seemed even
bigger, stronger, more menacing. She had to force
herself to keep from backing away.

He hesitated, his gaze raking over the cabin,
raking over her. He frowned at the candle.

She stood. It took all her bravery, but she stood,
forcing her eyes to meet his, to determine what was
there. There seemed to be nothing but a certain
coolness.

"I'm thirsty," she said. It came out as more of a challenge than a request, and she saw a quick flicker of something in his eyes. She hoped it was remorse, but that thought was quickly extinguished by his reply.

"Used to better places?" It was a sneer, plain and simple, and Shea felt anger stirring again.

"I'm used to gentlemen and simple . . . humanity."

"That's strange, considering your claim that you're Randall's daughter."

"I haven't claimed anything to you."

"That's right, you haven't," he agreed in a disagreeable voice. "You haven't said much at all."

"And I don't intend to. Not to a thief and a traitor."

"Be careful, Miss Randall. Your . . . continued health depends on this thief and traitor."

"That's supposed to comfort me?" Her tone was pure acid.

His gaze stabbed her. "You'll have to forgive me. I'm out of practice in trying to comfort anyone. Ten years out of practice."

"So you're going to starve me?"

"No," he said slowly. "I'm not going to do *that*."

The statement was ominous to Shea. "What are you going to do?"

"Follow my rules, and I won't do anything."

"You already are. You're keeping me here against my will."

He was silent for a moment, and Shea noted a muscle moving in his neck, as if he were just barely restraining himself.

"Lady, because of your . . . father, I was 'held'

against my will for ten years." She wanted to slap him for his mockery. She wanted to kick him where it would hurt the most. But now was not the time.

"Is that it? You're taking revenge out on me?"

The muscle in his cheek moved again. "No, Miss Randall, it's not that. You just happened to be in the wrong place at the wrong time. I don't have any more choices than you do." He didn't know why in the hell he was explaining, except her last charge galled him.

"You do."

He turned away from her. "Believe what you want," he said, his voice indifferent. "Blow out that candle and come with me if you want some water."

She didn't want to go with him, but she was desperate to shake her thirst. She blew out the candle, hoping that once outside he wouldn't see dried streaks of tears on her face. She didn't want to give him that satisfaction.

She didn't have to worry. He paid no attention to her, and she had to scurry to keep up with his long-legged strides. She knew she was plain, especially so in the loose-fitting britches and shirt she wore and with her hair in a braid. She also knew she should be grateful that he was indifferent to her, but a part of her wanted to goad him, confuse him . . . attract him.

Shea felt color flood her face. To restrain her train of thought, she concentrated on her surroundings.

Her horse was gone, although her belongings were propped against the tree stump. There was a shack to the left, and she noticed a lock on the door. That must be where he'd taken the weapons and where he kept his own horse. The keys must be in his pockets. He strode over to the building and picked up a bucket with his gloved hand.

She tried to pay attention to their route, but it seemed they had just melted into the woods and everything looked alike. She thought of turning around and running, but he was only a couple of feet ahead of her.

He stopped abruptly at a stream and leaned against a tree, watching her.

She had never drunk from a stream before, yet that was obviously what he expected her to do. The dryness in her mouth was worse, and she couldn't wait. She moved to the edge of the stream and kneeled, feeling awkward and self-conscious, knowing he was watching and judging. She scooped up a handful of water, then another, trying to sip it before it leaked through her fingers. She caught just enough to be tantalized.

She finally fell flat on her stomach and put her mouth in the water, taking long swallows of the icy cold water, mindless of the way the front of her shirt got soaked, mindless of anything but water.

It felt wonderful and tasted wonderful. When she was finally sated, she reluctantly sat up, and her gaze went to Tyler.

His stance was lazy but his eyes, like fine emeralds, were intense with fire. She felt a corresponding wave of heat consume her. She couldn't move her gaze from him, no matter how hard she tried. It was as if they were locked together.

He was the first to divert his gaze and his face settled quickly into its usual indifferent mask.

She looked down and noticed that her wet shirt clung to her, outlining her breasts. She swallowed hard and turned around. She splashed water on her face, hoping it would cool the heat suffusing her body.

She kept expecting Tyler to order her away, but he didn't. And she lingered as long as she could. She didn't want to go back to the dark cabin. She didn't want to face him, or those intense emotions she didn't understand.

She felt his gaze on her, and knew she should feel fear. He had been in prison a very long time. But she was certain he wouldn't touch her in a sexual way.

Because he despises you.

Because he despises your father.

She closed her eyes for a moment, and when she opened them, a spiral of light gleamed through the trees, hitting the stream. She wanted to reach out and catch that sunbeam, to climb it to some safe place.

But there were no safe places any longer.

She watched that ray of light until it slowly dissipated as the sun slipped lower in the sky, and then she turned around again. She hadn't expected such patience from Tyler.

"Ready?" he asked in his hoarse whisper.

The word held many meanings.

Ready for what? She wasn't ready for any of this.

But she nodded.

He sauntered over and offered his hand.

She refused it and rose by herself, stunned by how much she suddenly wanted to take his hand, to feel that strength again.

And Shea realized her battle wasn't entirely with him. It was also with herself.

"Susan Johnson brings sensuality to new
heights and beyond."
—*Romantic Times*

SUSAN JOHNSON
Nationally bestselling author of **Outlaw**
and **Silver Flame**

SEIZED BY LOVE
Now available in paperback

*Sweeping from the fabulous country estates and hunting
lodges to the opulent ballrooms and salons of the Russian
nobility, here is a novel of savage passions and dangerous
pleasures by the incomparable Susan Johnson, mistress of
the erotic historical.*

"*Under your protection?*" Alisa sputtered, flush-
ing vividly as the obvious and unmistakable clarity
of his explanation struck her. Of course, she should
have realized. How very stupid of her. The full
implication of what the public reaction to her
situation would be left her momentarily stunned,
devoured with shame. She was exceedingly thankful,
for the first time since her parents' death, that
they *weren't* alive to see the terrible depths to
which she had fallen, the sordid fate outlined for
her.

Irritated at the masterful certainty of Nikki's
assumption, and resentful to be treated once more

like a piece of property, she coldly said, "I don't recall placing myself under your protection."

"Come now, love," Nikki said reasonably, "if you recall, when I found you in that shed, your alternatives were surely limited; more severe beatings and possibly death if Forseus had continued drugging you. Hardly a choice of options, I should think. And consider it now," Nikki urged amiably, "plenty of advantages, especially if one has already shown a *decided* partiality for the man one has as protector. I'm not considered ungenerous, and if you contrive to please me in the future as well as you have to this date, we shall deal together quite easily."

Taking umbrage at his arrogant presumption that her role was to please *him*, Alisa indignantly said, "I haven't any *decided* partiality for you, you arrogant lecher, and furthermore—"

"Give me three minutes alone with you, my dear," Nikki interjected suavely, "and I feel sure I can restore my credit on that account."

Her eyes dropped shamefully before his candid regard, but she was angry enough to thrust aside the brief feeling of embarrassment, continuing belligerently. "Maria has some money of mine she brought with us. I'm not in *need* of protection."

"Not enough to buy you one decent gown, let alone support yourself, a child, and three servants," Nikki disagreed bluntly with his typical disregard for tact.

"Well, then," Alisa insisted heatedly, "I'm relatively well educated, young, and strong. I can obtain a position as governess."

"I agree in principle with your idea, but unfortunately, the pressures of existence in this world of travail serve to daunt the most optimistic hopes." His words were uttered in a lazy, mocking drawl. "For you, the role of governess"—the sarcasm in his voice was all too apparent—"is quite a pleasant conceit, my dear. You *will* forgive my speaking frankly, but I fear you are lacking in a sense of the realities of things.

"*If*—I say, *if*—any wife in her right mind would allow a provokingly beautiful young woman like yourself to enter her household, I'd wager a small fortune, the master of that house would be sharing your bed within the week. Consider the folly of the notion, love. At least with me there'd be no indignant wife to throw you and your retinue out into the street when her husband's preferences became obvious. And since I have a rather intimate knowledge of many of these wives, I think my opinion is to be relied upon. And as your protector," he continued equably, "I, of course, feel an obligation to maintain your daughter and servants in luxurious comfort."

"I am not a plaything to be bought!" Alisa said feelingly.

"Ah, my dear, but you are. Confess, it is a woman's role, primarily a pretty plaything for a man's pleasure and then inexorably as night follows day— a mother. Those are the two roles a woman plays. It's preordained. Don't fight it," he said practically.

Alisa would have done anything, she felt at that moment, to wipe that detestable look of smugness from Nikki's face.

"Perhaps I'll take Cernov up on his offer after all," she said with the obvious intent to provoke. "Is he richer than you? I must weigh the advantages if

I'm to make my way profitably in the demimonde," she went on calculatingly. "Since I'm merely a plaything, it behooves me to turn a practical frame of mind to the role of demirep and sell myself for the highest price in money and rank obtainable. I have a certain refinement of background—"

"Desist in the cataloguing if you please," he broke in rudely, and in a dangerously cold voice murmured, "Let us not cavil over trifles. You're staying with me." Alisa involuntarily quailed before the stark, open challenge in his eyes, and her heart sank in a most unpleasant way.

"So my life is a trifle?" she whispered, trembling with a quiet inner violence.

"You misunderstand, my dear," the even voice explained with just a touch of impatience. "It's simply that I don't intend to enter into any senseless wrangles or debates over your attributes and the direction in which your favors are to be bestowed. Madame, you're to remain my mistress." His lips smiled faintly but the smile never reached his eyes.

WILD CHILD
by Suzanne Forster
bestselling author of
SHAMELESS

"A storyteller of incandescent brilliance . . . beyond compare in a class by herself . . . that rare talent, a powerhouse writer whose extraordinary sensual touch can mesmerize . . ."
—*Romantic Times*

Her memorable characters and sizzling tales of romance and adventure have won her numerous awards and countless devoted readers. Now, with her trademark blend of intense sensuality and deep emotion, Suzanne Forster reunites adversaries who share a tangled past—and for whom an old spark of conflict will kindle into a dangerously passionate blaze . . .

"I want to talk about us," he said.

"Us?"

Blake could have predicted the stab of panic in her eyes, but he couldn't have predicted what was happening inside Cat. As she met his gaze, she felt herself dropping, a wind-rider caught in a powerful downdrift. The plummeting sensation in her stomach was sudden and sharp. The dock seemed to go out from under her feet, and as she imagined herself falling, she caught a glimpse of something in her mind that riveted her.

Surrender.

Even the glimpse of such naked emotion was terrifying to Cat. It entranced and enthralled her. It was the source of her panic. It was the wellspring of her deepest need. To be touched, to be loved. She shuddered in silence and raised her face to his.

By the time he did touch her, the shuddering was deep inside her. It was emotional and sexual and beautiful. No, she thought, this is impossible. This isn't happening. *Not with this man. Not with him . . .*

He curved his hand to her throat and drew her to him.

"What do I do, Cat?" he asked. "How do I make the sadness go away?"

The question rocked her softly, reverberating in the echo chamber her senses had become. *Not this man. Not him. He's hurt you too much. . . .*

"Sweet, sad, Cat." He caressed the underside of her chin with long, long strokes of his thumb. The sensations were soft and erotic and thrilling, and they accomplished exactly what they were supposed to, Cat realized, bringing her head up sharply. He wanted her to look up at him. He wanted her throat arched, her head tilted back.

No, Cat! He's hurt you too much.

"Don't," she whispered. "Not you . . ."

"Yes, Cat, me," he said. "It has to be me."

He bent toward her, and his lips touched hers with a lightning stroke of tenderness. Cat swallowed the moan in her throat. In all her guilty dreams of kissing Blake Wheeler—and there had been many—she had never imagined it as tender. She never had imagined a sweetness so sharp that it would fill her throat and tear through her heart like a poignant memory. Was this how lovers kissed? Lovers who had hurt each other and now needed to be very, very cautious? Lovers whose wounds weren't healed?

Age-old warnings stirred inside her. She should have resisted, she wanted to resist, but as his lips brushed over hers she felt yearnings flare up inside her—a wrenchingly sweet need to deepen the kiss, to be held and crushed in his arms. She had imagined him as self-absorbed, an egotistical lover who would take what he wanted and assume that being with him was enough for any woman. A night with Blake Wheeler. A night in heaven! She had imagined herself rejecting him, ordering him out of her bed and out of her life. She had imagined all of those things so many times . . . but never *tenderness*.

His mouth was warm. It was as vibrant as the water sparkling around them. She touched his arm, perhaps to push him away, and then his lips drifted over hers, and her touch became a caress. Her fingers shimmered over heat and muscle, and she felt a sudden, sharp need to be closer.

All of her attention was focused on the extraordinary thing that was happening to her. A kiss, she told herself, *it was just a kiss*. But he touched her with such rare tenderness. His fingers plucked at her nerve-strings as if she were a delicate musical instrument. His mouth transfused her with fire and drained her of energy at the same time. And when at last his arms came around her and brought her up against him, she felt a sweet burst of physical longing that saturated her senses.

She had dreamt of his body, too. And the feel of him now was almost more reality than she could stand. His thighs were steel, and his pelvic bones dug into her flesh. He was hard, righteously hard, and even the slightest shifts in pressure put her in touch with her own keening emptiness.

His tongue stroked her lips, and she opened

them to him slowly, irresistibly. On some level she knew she was playing a sword dance with her own emotions, tempting fate, tempting heartbreak, but the sensations were so exquisite, she couldn't stop herself. They seemed as inevitable and sensual as the deep currents swaying beneath them.

The first gliding touch of his tongue against hers electrified her. A gasp welled in her throat as he grazed her teeth and tingled sensitive surfaces. The penetration was deliciously languid and deep. By the time he lifted his mouth from hers, she was shocked and reeling from the taste of him.

The urge to push him away was instinctive.

"No, Cat," he said softly, inexplicably, "it's mine now. The sadness inside you is mine."

Studying her face, searching her eyes for something, he smoothed her hair and murmured melting suggestions that she couldn't consciously decipher. They tugged at her sweetly, hotly, pulling her insides to and fro, eliciting yearnings. Cat's first awareness of them was a kind of vague astonishment. It was deep and thrilling, what was happening inside her, like eddying water, like the sucking and pulling of currents. She'd never known such oddly captivating sensations.

The wooden dock creaked and the bay swelled gently beneath them, tugging at the pilings. Cat sighed as the rhythms of the sea and the man worked their enchantment. His hands *were* telepathic. They sought out all her tender spots. His fingers moved in concert with the deep currents, stroking the sideswells of her breasts, arousing her nerves to rivulets of excitement.

"Wild," he murmured as he cupped her breasts in his palms. "Wild, wild child."

And don't miss these spectacular
romances from Bantam Books,
on sale in May:

DARK JOURNEY
by the bestselling author
Sandra Canfield
"(Ms. Canfield's) superb style of writing
proves her to be an author extraordinaire."
—*Affaire de Coeur*

SOMETHING BORROWED SOMETHING BLUE
by
Jillian Karr
"Author Jillian Karr . . . explodes onto the
mainstream fiction scene . . . Great reading."
—*Romantic Times*

THE MOON RIDER
by the highly acclaimed
Virginia Lynn
"A master storyteller."
—*Rendezvous*

OFFICIAL RULES

To enter the sweepstakes below carefully follow all instructions found elsewhere in this offer.

The **Winners Classic** will award prizes with the following approximate maximum values: 1 Grand Prize: $26,500 (or $25,000 cash alternate); 1 First Prize: $3,000; 5 Second Prizes: $400 each; 35 Third Prizes: $100 each; 1,000 Fourth Prizes: $7.50 each. Total maximum retail value of Winners Classic Sweepstakes is $42,500. Some presentations of this sweepstakes may contain individual entry numbers corresponding to one or more of the aforementioned prize levels. To determine the Winners, individual entry numbers will first be compared with the winning numbers preselected by computer. For winning numbers not returned, prizes will be awarded in random drawings from among all eligible entries received. Prize choices may be offered at various levels. If a winner chooses an automobile prize, all license and registration fees, taxes, destination charges and, other expenses not offered herein are the responsibility of the winner. If a winner chooses a trip, travel must be complete within one year from the time the prize is awarded. Minors must be accompanied by an adult. Travel companion(s) must also sign release of liability. Trips are subject to space and departure availability. Certain black-out dates may apply.

The following applies to the sweepstakes named above:

No purchase necessary. You can also enter the sweepstakes by sending your name and address to: P.O. Box 508, Gibbstown, N.J. 08027. Mail each entry separately. Sweepstakes begins 6/1/93. Entries must be received by 12/30/94. Not responsible for lost, late, damaged, misdirected, illegible or postage due mail. Mechanically reproduced entries are not eligible. All entries become property of the sponsor and will not be returned.

Prize Selection/Validations: Selection of winners will be conducted no later than 5:00 PM on January 28, 1995, by an independent judging organization whose decisions are final. Random drawings will be held at 1211 Avenue of the Americas, New York, N.Y. 10036. Entrants need not be present to win. Odds of winning are determined by total number of entries received. Circulation of this sweepstakes is estimated not to exceed 200 million. All prizes are guaranteed to be awarded and delivered to winners. Winners will be notified by mail and may be required to complete an affidavit of eligibility and release of liability which must be returned within 14 days of date on notification or alternate winners will be selected in a random drawing. Any prize notification letter or any prize returned to a participating sponsor, Bantam Doubleday Dell Publishing Group, Inc., its participating divisions or subsidiaries, or the independent judging organization as undeliverable will be awarded to an alternate winner. Prizes are not transferable. No substitution for prizes except as offered or as may be necessary due to unavailability, in which case a prize of equal or greater value will be awarded. Prizes will be awarded approximately 90 days after the drawing. All taxes are the sole responsibility of the winners. Entry constitutes permission (except where prohibited by law) to use winners' names, hometowns, and likenesses for publicity purposes without further or other compensation. Prizes won by minors will be awarded in the name of parent or legal guardian.

Participation: Sweepstakes open to residents of the United States and Canada, except for the province of Quebec. Sweepstakes sponsored by Bantam Doubleday Dell Publishing Group, Inc., (BDD), 1540 Broadway, New York, NY 10036. Versions of this sweepstakes with different graphics and prize choices will be offered in conjunction with various solicitations or promotions by different subsidiaries and divisions of BDD. Where applicable, winners will have their choice of any prize offered at level won. Employees of BDD, its divisions, subsidiaries, advertising agencies, independent judging organization, and their immediate family members are not eligible.

Canadian residents, in order to win, must first correctly answer a time limited arithmetical skill testing question. Void in Puerto Rico, Quebec and wherever prohibited or restricted by law. Subject to all federal, state, local and provincial laws and regulations. For a list of major prize winners (available after 1/29/95): send a self-addressed, stamped envelope entirely separate from your entry to: Sweepstakes Winners, P.O. Box 517, Gibbstown, NJ 08027. Requests must be received by 12/30/94. DO NOT SEND ANY OTHER CORRESPONDENCE TO THIS P.O. BOX.

Don't miss these fabulous Bantam women's fiction titles

On Sale in May

DARK JOURNEY
by Sandra Canfield

"A masterful work."—Rendezvous

"Sandra Canfield...has penned an emotionally moving and thoroughly fascinating drama that captures both the essence of romance and the totality of the human spirit."
—Affaire de Coeur

_____56605-9 $5.50/$6.50 in Canada

SOMETHING BORROWED, SOMETHING BLUE
by Jillian Karr

Four weddings...Four women...Four lives on a collision course with violent passions and dangerous desires.

_____29990-5 $5.99/6.99 in Canada

THE MOON RIDER
by Virginia Lynn

A spellbinding new romance by the award-winning bestselling author Virginia Brown writing as Virginia Lynn.

"(Lynn's) novels shine with lively adventures, a special brand of humor, and sizzling romance."—Romantic Times

_____29693-0 $5.50/$6.50 in Canada

WHERE SHADOWS GO
by Eugenia Price

A stirring saga of love and friendship by the New York Times bestselling author of Bright Captivity.

_____56503-6 $6.50/$8.50 in Canada

Ask for these books at your local bookstore or use this page to order.

Bestselling Women's Fiction
Sandra Brown

_____	28951-9	TEXAS! LUCKY	$5.99/6.99 in Canada
_____	28990-X	TEXAS! CHASE	$5.99/6.99
_____	29500-4	TEXAS! SAGE	$5.99/6.99
_____	29085-1	22 INDIGO PLACE	$5.99/6.99
_____	29783-X	A WHOLE NEW LIGHT	$5.99/6.99
_____	56045-X	TEMPERATURES RISING	$5.99/6.99
_____	56274-6	FANTA C	$4.99/5.99
_____	56278-9	LONG TIME COMING	$4.99/5.99

Amanda Quick

_____	28354-5	SEDUCTION	$5.99/6.99
_____	28932-2	SCANDAL	$5.99/6.99
_____	28594-7	SURRENDER	$5.99/6.99
_____	29325-7	RENDEZVOUS	$5.99/6.99
_____	29316-8	RECKLESS	$5.99/6.99
_____	29316-8	RAVISHED	$4.99/5.99
_____	29317-6	DANGEROUS	$5.99/6.99
_____	56506-0	DECEPTION	$5.99/7.50

Nora Roberts

_____	29078-9	GENUINE LIES	$5.99/6.99
_____	28578-5	PUBLIC SECRETS	$5.99/6.99
_____	26461-3	HOT ICE	$5.99/6.99
_____	26574-1	SACRED SINS	$5.99/6.99
_____	27859-2	SWEET REVENGE	$5.99/6.99
_____	27283-7	BRAZEN VIRTUE	$5.99/6.99
_____	29597-7	CARNAL INNOCENCE	$5.50/6.50
_____	29490-3	DIVINE EVIL	$5.99/6.99

Iris Johansen

_____	29871-2	LAST BRIDGE HOME	$4.50/5.50
_____	29604-3	THE GOLDEN BARBARIAN	$4.99/5.99
_____	29244-7	REAP THE WIND	$4.99/5.99
_____	29032-0	STORM WINDS	$4.99/5.99
_____	28855-5	THE WIND DANCER	$4.95/5.95
_____	29968-9	THE TIGER PRINCE	$5.50/6.50
_____	29944-1	THE MAGNIFICENT ROGUE	$5.99/6.99
_____	29945-X	BELOVED SCOUNDREL	$5.99/6.99

Ask for these titles at your bookstore or use this page to order.

Please send me the books I have checked above. I am enclosing $ _____ (add $2.50 to cover postage and handling). Send check or money order, no cash or C. O. D.'s please.

Mr./ Ms. _____

Address _____

City/ State/ Zip _____

Send order to: Bantam Books, Dept. FN 16, 2451 S. Wolf Road, Des Plaines, IL 60018

Please allow four to six weeks for delivery.

Prices and availability subject to change without notice.